Broken Rules

Marie Tuhart

Hot Blooded Press

BROKEN RULES

QUALITY CONTROL: We strive to produce error-free books, but even with all the eyes that see the story during the production process, slips get by. So please, if you find a typo or any formatting issues, please let us know at marie@marietuhart.com so that we may correct it.

Thank you!

Blurb

♥

After Becca Dalton catches her fiancé in bed with her boss,she dumps them both and walks away from the life she thought she wanted.Heartbroken and jobless, she seeks refuge at Quick Silver Ranch, hoping for alittle peace before figuring out her next move.

But Becca's fresh start takes a steamy detour when she realizes she's accidentally signed up for a week at an exclusive fantasy retreat—where adventurous couples explore their deepest desires. The only problem? She needs a partner to stay.

Enter Tyler Carson, her ruggedly sexy, never-forgotten college ex. A cowboy with a sinful smile and a dominant streak, Tyler is more than willing to step in—and tie her up in ways she never imagined. For one week, he'll take charge, push every boundary, and remind Becca exactly what she's been missing.

But as the nights heat up and their past collides with the present, Tyler has only one goal—convince this city girl to stop running and finally stake her claim... right by his side.

Acknowledgements

♥

Laurie, the best writer friend one can have.

Red Quill Editing team, you are the best team to work with.

Publisher's Note: No Artificial Intelligence was used in the writing of this book.

Contents

Chapter One

♥

Becca Dalton threw her suitcase and the check-in packet on the colorful quilt in her cabin at the Quick Silver Ranch and dug out her sneakers. The concierge had been insistent that she read and sign several forms—probably all kinds of release of liability paperwork— but she managed to persuade the very persistent, determined woman to give her a couple of hours to settle in by swearing up, down, and sideways, that she'd turn in the paperwork after she read it in the quiet of her room.

Even with the promise of wading through that packet, she needed to get outside. Now.

Dispensing with her high heels in favor of the sneakers, she didn't even want to stop to change clothes or take her hair down instead of leaving it in a bun. She strode from the cabin that would be her home for the next nine days and found one of the walking trails she'd been told about when she arrived. The fresh air brushed her skin as she briskly walked.

Birds chirped in the trees, and the leaves rustled in the light breeze. She didn't have a clue where the trail led, and at this point, she didn't care. *Slow down.* Her steps slowed. No need to be in a hurry here. Becca stopped and took a deep breath.

Scents came to life. Clean air, not city air. Her shoulders relaxed as the tension melted away.

Life had thrown her too many curve balls, and she needed a break. Too much had happened just in the last few days. She'd not only found her fiancé, Alan, in bed with her boss, but he'd been lying about his sexual orientation and using her for cover. She called her wedding off, quit her job and interviewed for her dream job.

Becca wasn't sure if she should celebrate or cry. Nothing made sense anymore, including this trip her best friend, Angie, convinced her to take. Hell, Angie had paid for it, saying it was a pre-wedding present.

This trip would be a chance for Becca to find herself and start over.

But at a dude ranch located no more than a two-hour drive from San Francisco? She chuckled in spite of her mood. Angie had told her to take a romantic trip with Alan.

Now, that wasn't possible. Hell, he wasn't even the outdoorsy type. He couldn't stand the sight of an ant in his apartment, and his skin was whiter than a vampire's.

Her fingers slipped inside the pocket of her designer suit. Damn, no cell phone. Rules to ensure privacy, she was told at check-in.

Becca took a deep breath. Being unplugged was probably a good thing. She wouldn't have to deal with texts from her mother, and Alan couldn't call to beg for forgiveness or offer explanations.

Not that she'd forgive that lying, cheating rat. It was bad enough he'd cheated on her—and with her boss, no less—but the utter depths of the lies compounded the betrayal.

The best thing was the phone call she received right before turning her phone in. She'd landed the job she'd interviewed for. She really wanted to talk to Angie and convince her to join her at the ranch. This week would be so much more fun if she had a friend with her.

She took another deep breath and let it out. This was her time to chill out, explore nature, and not worry about anyone or anything. When was the last time she did something like that? College, maybe?

When a strange noise caught her attention, she slowed her steps as she continued to follow the path when it turned. A neigh. She now recognized the sound, and as she cleared the trees, she spotted the horse.

A wishful sigh escaped her. She'd always wanted to learn how to ride. Her mother refused to let her when she was a child, and now, as an adult, she hadn't made the time. Maybe this week she could make it her priority.

Her gaze switched from the horse to the man next to the animal.

Oh my! What a man. Her gaze roamed over him, taking in his semi-short midnight hair, past broad shoulders, to ass and legs encased in denim, all the way to his black cowboy boots. Reversing course, she settled on his large hands and long fingers as they stroked the mare's neck in such a loving way. Almost as if he was caressing the animal's skin, letting the horse know he'd take care of her, and she was safe.

What would it feel like to have those hands on her body, her breasts, to have those long, strong fingers in her pussy, pumping them in and out, bringing her to climax?

Need rose in her. Good. She wasn't dead. Heck, she wasn't even broken-hearted. Alan hadn't broken her heart, only bruised her pride, and shouldn't that tell her something? Maybe all along she'd known Alan wasn't the man for her. After the break-up, she realized she'd never really been emotionally invested in their relationship.

The man's voice was low as he spoke to the horse, but there was something familiar about his deep timbre, as if she'd heard it before. Without thought, her gaze traveled again to the finest ass she'd seen a long time, the faded denim caressing him when he shifted his stance.

"Would you like to meet Rose?"

Her heart jumped, and her head snapped up. Darn if he didn't look familiar. But she couldn't place him.

"I didn't mean to disturb you," she said, willing her racing heart to slow down.

He turned his head, and she noticed a hint of stubble, a slightly crooked nose, and thick lashes any woman would kill to have. His raven hair had a wind tossed look to it. And as his blue eyes locked on her, her nerves tingled, and her nipples hardened. She'd never had a reaction like this to a man before, not just from one look.

"Hop over the fence, and I'll introduce you."

Hop over? Yeah, right. "How does one *hop over* this fence?" She gazed at the wood railings, then looked down at the work suit she hadn't taken the time to change out of.

Her breath caught in her throat when he strode over to her.

He laughed, making her shiver. "It's easy. Put your left foot on the lower board."

Becca did as he said. His tone softened, becoming almost intimate. "Now stand up and throw your right leg over the top."

"Isn't there another way?" Her throat tightened as she looked around for a gate.

"This is much more fun." He moved closer to the fence. His woodsy scent mixed with pure masculine heat. "I'll help you."

Swallowing at his nearness, she pulled herself up and threw her leg over. She squealed when his hands closed around her waist, and her fingers dug into his shoulders as he lifted her over the fence.

"There. Wasn't that better than walking around?" He set her on her feet, amusement in his voice.

She tilted her head back and gazed into his twinkling blue eyes. When he chuckled, her body went on high alert.

She knew that laugh! Tyler Carson. The bad boy of Jackson High and her college lover.

Her knees weakened and her heart pounded.

Oh my God. This was the last thing she expected. Although they'd parted on good terms, she hadn't seen Tyler in years... and he still looked good. She kept her gaze on his face. Was he as surprised to see her as she was to see him? She couldn't tell.

Becca caught herself before she checked her hair. Tyler had seen her tousled after making love to her for half the night. And while that was years ago, she didn't think she'd changed that much.

I wonder if he's still single. Tension coiled in her gut. That didn't matter because she wasn't here to start a new relationship. She didn't need the heartbreak. But the memory of his touch called out to her, and she wanted to answer that call. How would she survive a week with him around if her body was already out of control with just a look and a touch?

***

Tyler Carson couldn't prevent the grin spreading across his face. He was aware new guests were arriving at Quick Silver Ranch today but seeing Becca was a surprise.

A pleasant one. He had just lifted the woman he should have never let go over the fence and back into his life.

He hadn't seen her since he left San Francisco for Humboldt State. Several inches shorter than his own six-foot three frame, Becca still packed a punch to his libido. When he lifted her over the fence, she weighed next to nothing. The average newborn filly weighed more than she did.

It wasn't as if he hadn't been alerted to her presence when she walked into the paddock. Leaves and branches had crunched under her shoes. He'd been surprised since most guests didn't venture out to the stables to go for a ride, at least not until the second or third day of their stay.

He was still holding her waist when he caught the scent of jasmine and his cock hardened. The reaction caught him off guard, and he knew he needed to let her go before he did something foolish.

Like carry her into the stable, throw her into a freshly bedded stall, and thrust himself deep into her pussy.

He remembered how good that felt, even after all this time.

Behave.

Then it smacked him like taking a hoof to the groin: Becca was a guest, and that meant she was off limits. Besides, this was a ranch for couples—no one came solo.

Fighting his instincts, he released her and stepped back. "It's been a long time, Becca."

Too long.

"Good to see you again, Tyler." She ran a hand over her hips, and he took note of the business suit, sans jacket, she was wearing.

"You *do* remember me." That pleased him in ways he couldn't name. He sauntered to Rose as if he didn't have a care in the world, even though he wanted to remove the hairpins holding Becca's light brown hair and watch it tumble around her shoulders. His lips tingled with anticipation of tasting her rosy-red mouth.

No, don't think like that. Off limits, remember? There were rules he had to obey.

"How could I forget the bad boy of Jackson High, the captain and quarterback of the championship San Francisco State football team?"

Not to mention we were lovers. Everything else she said was true, but she left out their college romance.

Then again, since the ranch was for couples, *I wonder if her guy even knows about me? Maybe she doesn't want him to know.*

He glanced at her left hand. No ring, but she had to be here with someone. Single people were not allowed at the ranch.

"Have you been around horses before, Becca?" He craved to hold her close. Tyler looked toward the sky. He shouldn't be thinking this way. There had to be a man waiting for her, or she wouldn't be here.

"Not unless you count a pony when I was ten."

"When you're ready, walk around her head to stand here." He'd let her make the decision to approach. "I'll introduce you to Rose, Becca."

Why do I keep saying her name? Maybe because some-where deep inside he couldn't believe she was here? He wanted nothing more than to remind her of the fact he was her first lover.

Reining in his libido, he fought to remember why people came to the ranch.

Her dark blue suit looked out of place. Dressed for success, his ex would have said. Another reason he should keep his distance. She looked polished, professional, a far cry from his Becca in college. She looked like a city woman now, and city women were not for him.

When she walked around to him, her heat soaked into his skin and Tyler inhaled jasmine again. She'd loved jasmine shampoo when they were together and apparently still did. Memories rushed back, and he let them soak into his psyche, reliving the good times they had together.

"Rose is a beautiful horse." Her voice was soft with a tiny bit of hesitation in it.

Forcing his mind back to his task, Tyler reached down and snagged her hand. Still as soft as ever. "She's a beautiful four-year-old with impeccable bloodlines." Becca trembled beneath his touch. Was she afraid of the horse or him?

Lifting her hand, he placed her palm against Rose's withers and kept his on top of it. "Stroke her neck with easy, gentle movements. Like this."

Rose snorted, and Becca flinched against him, jerking her hand free.

"Easy." His arms automatically slipped around Becca's waist, anchoring her to him. She fit perfectly against him. So few women did.

"Did I scare her?"

"No, she liked it. She only snorted. Go ahead, pet her again." Keeping her anchored against him, he watched her raise her hand and run her fingers over Rose's coat.

His cock pulsed, remembering those same fingers stroking him, up and down, varying the pressure as she went from base to tip.

Damn, this isn't good. He shifted his stance. The last thing he needed was for her to feel his hard-on.

"She's very soft."

"I groom her every day. It keeps her coat shiny and smooth."

"It must be nice to have your hair brushed every day." There was a wistful tone in her voice.

I'd brush your hair every day, if you wanted.

But he didn't say that. "Rose likes it." His gaze took in Becca's hair, pulled into a severe bun. He wondered if her hair was as long as it had been in college—or was it longer? When they made love, it would brush against his skin.

He released her waist with his left hand, then stopped himself. He almost reached up and removed the pins to see, but at the last second stopped himself. *What am I doing?* Why was Becca effecting him this way? There had been beautiful women on the ranch before, but he'd never been tempted to make a pass at any of them.

Even when they indicated they were open to having him as a lover. With every ounce of strength, he released her and stepped away.

"Who would I see about taking riding lessons while I'm here?" she asked.

"I can teach you." *Oh yeah*, his cock shouted in approval. He'd teach her to ride all right. "After dinner tonight, we'll set something up." He was digging himself one hell of a hole, but maybe after meeting her partner that would cool his libido. "Speaking of dinner"—he glanced at his watch—"I need to put Rose back in her stall and clean up."

"Of course." She slid away from him, and he missed her already. *Get a grip.*

"I'll help you back over the fence." It would be smarter to have her walk through the stable area, but she was wearing sneakers, not really great for the stables. He escorted her to the fence and helped her climb back over.

"Thank you, Tyler." She tilted her head as she looked up at him. "It's good to see you again. I'll see you around." The sway of her hips as she strode away made him want her even more.

"It's impossible," he muttered.

***

Becca thought about Tyler as she made her way back to her cabin. What were the odds of running into him? Astronomical, but that didn't stop her from thinking about how delicious he looked.

More filled out than their college days, more handsome, more muscular, and damn, if he still didn't make her panties wet. She'd forgotten how much Tyler always did that to her.

Yes, finding Alan in bed with her boss had been difficult, as was calling off the wedding and quitting her job. Still, that incident set off a chain of decisions she'd procrastinated about for too long.

She'd suspected Alan wasn't the right man for her for the last eight months, but she'd gone along with the engagement party and the wedding planning to avoid making waves with her mother. The expression on Alan's face when she walked in on them didn't come close to her shock and disbelief, followed by anger, followed by a mixture of numbness, comprehension...

And relief.

The scene played out in her mind like a badly written movie script. Alan's stunned expression, Rupert fumbling to cover himself. Staring at Alan, then Rupert. Taking off the engagement ring and putting it on the dresser. Hearing herself tell Alan she was relieved to finally understand why he wasn't interested in sex with her. Then there was the almost unnatural calm that followed the jumbled emotions she still couldn't sort out. "Go live your life and be your true self, Alan. If you'd been honest, we could've been friends." She turned and left the room, still surprised her legs hadn't turned to jelly. The doorknob turning as she opened the door to leave the apartment. "And Rupert, bag of shit that you are and always will be, I quit."

Becca blinked when she found herself standing in front of her cabin. She'd been so lost in thought she didn't realize she'd walked the whole way back. Today was a new start. That meant not thinking so much. Thinking too much was what spun her into the engagement to Alan. Her brain wasn't exactly doing a great job with men, so maybe she should follow her body.

Tyler. Her body tingled. Yes, they'd been lovers in college and had fun together, but then went their separate ways.

Now? They were different people, but she still desired him and his touch and nearness still weakened her knees.

She glanced at the clock. An hour. One hour to get ready for dinner. In that time, she would have to make a choice. Follow her mind, which told her she was on the rebound, or follow her desires?

This won't be easy.

Chapter Two

♥

At six on the nose, Becca strode into the dining room of the main ranch house. She couldn't believe how quick time slipped by now that she'd come to some conclusions about her life and her needs.

Smiling, she glanced around the room. She was greeted by six people sitting at the table. They all looked like couples, and she fought against squirming with anxiety because she was alone. Her stomach tightened, and she had to remind herself that she didn't need to feel out of place because she was single. There was nothing wrong with it.

She was about to pull a chair out when her nerves tingled.

"Allow me."

Tyler. Only his voice could make her pussy cream like that. "Thank you."

"You're welcome." His breath brushed against her ear as she sat. A shiver of excitement traveled through her body.

Lord, he could still arouse her with his voice. Hadn't she been reminded of that at the stable? Then his heat cooled as he took his place on her left. That was when she spotted a man she hadn't noticed before at the other end of the table.

He grinned from ear to ear. "Welcome, everyone," he said. "I'm Jared, and at the opposite end is my business partner, Tyler. We want to welcome you to Quick Silver Ranch."

Jared glanced around the table, his gaze lingering on the empty chair on Becca's right.

I wonder if they're missing a guest.

"If you need anything," he continued. "All you have to do is ask. We will do our best to provide you with whatever you desire."

Laughter floated in the air, but Becca wasn't sure why.

"I can't wait to try out what you're providing," the man on Tyler's right said.

More laughter.

"We'll do our best to keep up with you," Jared said. "Tonight is a chance for everyone to get acquainted. Tomorrow, your adventure starts."

As if on cue, a large man and several other people carried bowls and platters of food into the dining room. The smell of roast beef and freshly baked bread made Becca's mouth water.

When was the last time I ate? Last night?

Plates were filled, and everyone began introducing themselves over the wonderful food. Becca found she was right: The others were all couples, and one of the couples had stayed at the ranch before.

Then it was her turn, and all eyes focused on her. "I'm Becca. My best friend gifted me this trip to the ranch, and I'm looking forward to the experience."

"Is your partner joining you later?" Jared asked.

"Partner?" Her gaze sought Tyler before returning to Jared. "I'm here alone."

Silence descended. Becca drew a deep breath as she kept her gaze on Jared.

Why is he looking like there's something wrong? Because, based on the confusion and concern in Jared's expression, oh yes, there was definitely something wrong.

"This shouldn't have happened," Jared muttered.

She looked around the table, briefly studying each person, and each face held an element of shock or surprise.

Oh, no. Something was definitely wrong. The food in her stomach turned into a lead ball. *Maybe coming here alone wasn't such a good idea.*

Angie hadn't mentioned it was for couples only. She said it was a dude ranch, but now it seemed like it was more. Was this what the lady at check-in meant? *I need to read that packet.*

Becca swallowed, trying to stop the panic welling inside her. She really wanted to have this week away from the stress and tension of the city. And maybe to explore being reunited with Tyler, but now...

Not waiting to find out what she'd done wrong or why everyone was looking at her funny, Becca carefully slid her chair back. She hated being the odd man out. "Excuse me." She turned and fled the room as she fought back tears.

Why does life keep throwing me curve balls?

Chapter Three

♥

Tyler started to rise before he dropped back into his chair. He couldn't go after her. Not until he and Jared talked.

A part of him was ecstatic she was alone on this trip. It meant he didn't have any competition for her time, but complications remained.

The ranch was meant for couples; Becca was here alone.

His gut tightened. If Jared wanted her to leave, there wasn't anything Tyler could do.

"Oh, my," Emma, one of the guests, said. "The poor thing."

"It'll be okay." Tyler forced a smile. "I'll go talk with Becca in a bit, and we'll get this straightened out."

Still, Tyler barely held his impatience in check as dinner ended and dessert was consumed. Finally, the couples began to wander off.

"My office, Tyler," Jared said before striding out of the room.

Tyler followed his business partner. Becca being here alone meant a long conversation with Jared.

How'd this slip through the cracks? Their website was exceptionally clear that the ranch was for couples only.

Even so, he wanted Becca to stay so they could pick up where they'd left off in college.

"This isn't supposed to happen," Jared said, closing the door behind Tyler and running his free hand through his brown hair.

"I know." Tyler and Jared had safeguards in place, but somehow they failed. If Becca was here alone, would she be interested in pairing with him? His dick liked that thought. They'd played around a bit back in college, but was she even into what he'd grown to love? Tyler rubbed his chin. "I'll go talk with Becca. It's not like we can't handle a single person wanting to take advantage of a regular dude ranch."

"True, but we're an adult ranch. What happens if she wanders upon another couple? Or into one of the special cabins? Or a classroom?"

"The special cabins are locked for a reason. The classrooms, we control them." Tyler tried to make light of the situation because Jared had a right to be concerned. When they went into this business five years ago, they'd agreed the ranch was for couples only.

Fully consenting couples.

"As for seeing another couple, some might like it, but Becca might not. I'll explain to her and let her make her decision."

Jared stared at him.

Tyler took a breath, knowing he needed to explain better why he wanted Becca to stay. "I know Becca. We went to high school and college together." He wasn't going to lie or conceal anything from Jared, they were as close as brothers. "And we were lovers."

"I see."

"I know we have a hands-off policy with the guests, but—"

"You want her."

Tyler nodded.

Jared blew out a breath. "Go and talk to her. Tell her about the adult activities of the ranch. She hasn't turned in the paperwork in the check-in packet. Make absolutely sure she understands it completely, thoroughly. Then, if she wants to stay and be with you, we can make an exception. In the meantime, I'll talk with the intake staff. They should have caught this."

"Thanks." Tyler relaxed. "I know this is unusual for us."

"Yeah. I only want what is best for the ranch."

Tyler nodded.

"But if she wants to leave, you have to let her go. We'll give her a full refund."

"She'll stay." He felt confident she would. There was still a sexual attraction between them. He'd felt it at the stables, and he was sure she had too. But Jared was right about one thing: He couldn't pressure Becca into staying.

No matter how much he craved her.

***

"Angie, I'm going to kill you," Becca muttered, back in her cabin. On the table in front of her were the contents of the packet she'd thrown on the bed. A book about the ranch with a map of the grounds and a list of activities. And several forms: NDA, release of liability, and declaration of consent. Is this what Angie's cryptic comments about 'activities' meant?

Adult activities. Activities meant for couples.

She jumped to her feet and began pacing. Why had Angie sent her to an adult ranch? Had she known the activities were sexual?

No, that didn't make sense. Did Angie think this place would loosen Alan up? And why insist that I come alone after the breakup?

Damn, I need my cell. Maybe the ranch house had a phone she could use.

Couples only. Becca wouldn't have come if she'd known. All Angie told her was that it was a dude ranch. *Angie wouldn't have sent me here alone if she'd known it was couples only. Would she?* Becca knew her best friend. *I told her I didn't want to go to the ranch. But nooooo; she insisted.* "It'll be fun," she said. "Relax. Recharge. Embrace the new start and new job."

God, she's devious.

The two of them got a bit drunk when Becca called off her engagement, and they'd talked about sex and fantasies. Angie told Becca she needed to relax, let Mother Nature take control, and have fun with a nice cowboy on the ranch.

Short-lived excitement sent shivers over her skin. She didn't *have* a partner.

A twinge of sadness flowed through her.

What about Tyler? What was he thinking? She was here alone, all alone. *Does he think I did it on purpose?* That didn't make sense. She hadn't even known he'd be here.

But now a crazy idea popped into her head and her core clenched.

How would Tyler feel if I ask him to be my partner this week? No, that wasn't possible. She paced from the fireplace to the patio doors. She'd read about the variety of activities, and her body still felt aflame with the possibilities. As each one flashed through her mind, the man standing in front of her wasn't Alan.

It was Tyler. Strong, capable, great-in-bed Tyler.

Becca rested her head against the door, frustrated emotionally, mentally, and now physically.

Why is this happening now? Would it be a bad idea to ask Tyler?

Her mind didn't know, even as her body heated.

What were the risks? Rejection for sure. Disappointment, maybe.

Elation if he said yes.

Her mind played through all the possibilities.

Tyler was one of the owners, and she'd bet money there was a rule prohibiting him from getting involved with a guest. Hell, this whole thing was set up for couples in a relationship, not for once-upon-a-time lovers.

Her choices were limited.

Actually, there was only one—leave. Her body wanted her to stay, but her mind was aware of the risks. It was better to play it safe and leave. Becca went to the window and looked out, her guts churning.

Isn't that what I always do? Play it safe? She'd done it with Alan. *Look where that got me.*

Indecision kept her from going into the bedroom and packing.

Then a knock on the front door pulled her out of her thoughts. Crossing the room, she opened the door.

"Hi," Tyler said.

Her insides melted at seeing him there, heat rose in her cheeks.

If he only knew what I'd just been thinking... Liquid fire flooded her body, and her nipples grew hard. It wasn't fair that he could do this to her after all this time.

"Come in." She left the door open and retreated, sliding her hands into her jeans pockets.

He closed the door with a quiet *click* even as she paced around the room.

"I didn't realize... I mean... Oh, hell." She waved her hands in the air as she tried to explain. "I'm sorry. I'll leave."

"You don't have to." He crossed the room and stopped in front of her.

The heat coming from his body singed her skin. "It's couples only. I didn't know about the adult part either until I read the rules just now."

"It is usually couples only. But you do have a choice in the matter."

"I don't see how." She tilted her head and stared at him. *Does he want me to stay?*

"We do have regular dude ranch activities. I'm sure you read that in the brochure. I can teach you to ride, if you decide to stay. I can be your guide for the week."

"That might work."

Who am I kidding? Yes, it would work, but it would also be torture. He was asking as a friend, not as a lover.

An unwanted, disconcerting feeling overwhelmed her. Even after all this time, she still had a compelling attraction to Tyler. It gave her more proof that marrying Alan would have been a big mistake.

"Or," he continued, "you *could* participate in all the ranch has to offer. With me as your partner." He stood there, not touching her, apparently giving her space. "It's your choice, Becca."

What do I have to lose? She wanted to feel like a woman again, and Tyler could do that for her, if he was willing.

"I want you to know before we do anything that I'm not on the rebound. My ex-fiancé and I were never intimate." Her gaze met with his. She let out a breath she didn't realize she had been holding when he didn't respond.

I want to stay. Her mind was made up. She stepped closer. "Yes, I'll be your partner."

Chapter Four

B ecca stared at Tyler, not quite believing he'd asked her to stay and be his partner for the adult activities. Her heart pounded as the air vibrated with anticipation and silence. Breathing was difficult. What was he thinking?

Tyler stepped behind her, his strong hands curving around her shoulders even as he pressed his hard body against her back. His palms skimmed over her arms, leaving shivers of anticipation until his hands settled on her waist.

"I'm happy you've decided to stay and be my partner." His breath brushed against her ear.

"Are you sure this is what you want? I don't want you to feel like you've been forced."

He shook his head. "I want you here. Fate saw fit to send you back into my life, and I'm going to take full advantage of it." He turned her in his embrace. "For the record, I've never partnered with a guest here at the ranch. This is a one-time deal. Only with you."

Something wild and wanton built in her. "That's good to know." She fought to keep her hands at her side rather than sinking them into his raven hair and pulling his lips down to hers. What was it about Tyler that made her lose all common sense?

"You know it'll be good between us." His lips brushed her cheek, sending a streak of fire through her veins. "It was always good between us."

His lips skimmed the corner of hers. In that instant, she decided to hell with it. She would jump into the deep end. She reached up and curved her fingers around his neck.

When his mouth took hers, her lips parted and his tongue invaded. His kiss felt familiar, yet new. They were different people now. Older, more mature.

Her tongue played with his, and she tasted a hint of chocolate and something else.

A flavor she'd tasted before only with him. Now it was richer, deeper. His tongue stroked along the roof of her mouth as he tasted her.

She tightened her grip on him—she wanted him.

Their tongues tangled and dueled as the kiss lasted, lingered. Passion rose in her as her body came alive while wrapped around his.

Was it always like this before? She didn't think it had ever been this hot, this passionate, this needy. This was more sensual, more...everything.

Becca squirmed in his arms as she tried to maneuver against him. He held her firm as the kiss continued. Until he lifted his head and she moaned in protest.

He gazed down at her. "Think about what we'll be exploring—all things sensual and sexual together. I don't want you doing this on impulse and regretting it later." He kissed her one final time, hard and fast. Before she even had time to process it, he turned and walked out, gently closing the door behind him, leaving her swaying on her feet.

Didn't she need time to think about everything? There was danger in the deep end. Her fingers touched her lips, the feel of his kiss still there.

Nope. The water's just fine.

Chapter Five

♥

Becca walked into the dining room of the main house the next morning, looking for Tyler. She was surprised to see Jared sitting alone at the table with a cup of coffee and a tablet in front of him.

"Good morning, Becca," he said.

"Morning." Going over to the buffet, she poured herself some coffee and took a seat at the table, disappointed Tyler wasn't there. She stared down at her coffee, unsure how Jared felt about her being there.

"I'm sorry if you felt uncomfortable last night," Jared said.

Her head snapped up to see Jared watching her. Could he tell she hadn't slept? She'd put on more make-up than usual this morning.

"At dinner," he added.

She released her breath. "Not your fault. My friend didn't tell me about the adult part of the ranch, or that it was for couples only."

"Having couples makes things easier." He cleared his throat. "Tyler told me last night what happened and why you didn't know it was couples only. And that you want to stay."

Heat flooded her cheeks. She really had nothing to be embarrassed about. Staying meant leaving her inhibitions behind, but hearing it said out loud made it seem...

She wasn't sure. Risqué maybe. "If it'll cause a problem—"

"It won't. You'll be good for Tyler. I haven't seen that sparkle in his eyes in a long time. You shook his world up, and I'm glad." Jared rose, rounded the table, and stood next to her. "Just make him work for it," he said softly.

She was about to ask what he meant when Tyler walked in. Her heart pounded, her nipples tightened, and damned if her pussy didn't tingle with excitement. She watched him as he poured himself a cup of coffee, blew on it, took a sip, and then walked over to take the empty seat next to her.

Oh yes, Tyler looked good enough to eat. Jeans molded to his hips and legs, a white T-shirt stretched across his broad shoulders, and hair mussed. She barely registered Jared leaving the room.

"Any second thoughts?" His voice was husky, as if he'd just woken up.

Jared's advice of making Tyler work for it echoed in her brain. "Straight to the point, are we?"

He'd never seemed this authoritative before.

I like it. A lot. She shifted, and their legs touched. Awareness shot through her at the innocent touch. Her body confirmed the decision she'd made in the wee hours of the morning.

"No second thoughts. I'm in for whatever you can throw at me."

And there was the grin she remembered so well. Perfectly matched his bad-boy persona. Both in and out of bed, he'd claimed her attention.

His palm brushed over her thigh, and she swore a bolt of lightning tore through her body.

Becca picked up her mug and took the last sip of barely warm coffee, trying to control her body's reaction to him. She needed to keep her cool here.

"We need to discuss what services you'd like to use while you're here," he said.

She fumbled her mug and it clattered to the table. Thank goodness it was empty; otherwise, there would've been coffee everywhere.

He glanced at the table, one eyebrow just the slightest bit higher than the other. "But first, I want you to eat breakfast." He stood. "I'll gather some materials for us to go over and meet you in your cabin in thirty minutes."

"Aren't you going to eat?"

"I already have." He sauntered out of the room.

Her gaze followed him. Damn, he had a fine ass. Becca closed her eyes. It wouldn't be easy to make Tyler work for it as Jared suggested. Her body was already on fire for him, every nerve on alert for his touch.

Shaking her head, she stood and got some breakfast from the buffet. If she was going to tangle with the bad boy, she would need her strength.

Because I plan to be a very bad girl.

***

Thirty minutes later, Becca paced the living room of her small cabin. She'd finally found an MP3 player because the silence had been driving her up a wall. That problem solved, now only her body was driving her crazy.

Alive. Her body was alive and kicking, craving the one man who set her on fire faster than matches to dry tinder.

How will I cope?

It wasn't like they hadn't had sex before, but that was back in college. So why did this feel so different? They were adults at an adult ranch where anything went as long as they both consented to it.

How do I really feel about that? She paused her pacing, unsure. Scared? Excited? Was she staying on the ranch for the right reasons? Yes, she decided. It was time for her to shed what her life had become in the last five years and free the real woman inside.

A sharp knock startled her out of her thoughts. Taking a deep breath to settle her racing heart, she opened the door.

Tyler filled the doorway. With a shaking breath, Becca stepped back as he stepped into the room. He turned, shut the door, and the *snick* of the lock echoed in the room.

Every nerve in her body flashed on high alert. When his gaze captured hers, she forgot how to breathe. His eyes turned from blue to midnight with desire as he stood there, legs apart and arms crossed over his chest.

There's the bad boy I remember. The adventurous man who would take her places she'd never been before.

"How did you sleep last night?" he asked.

"What?" She shook her head, taking a breath before her lungs shut down. Once the oxygen reached her brain his question registered. "I didn't. I couldn't think about anything but us." *Now why did I have to blurt that out?*

"Good. I wasn't alone then." She had to tilt her head back as he walked over to her. She'd forgotten how much taller he was than her. "Why don't we go outside to the back patio and talk? We have some things to discuss before we start."

Tyler didn't wait for her to answer. He took her hand and gently tugged, guiding her outside to one of the high-backed patio chairs. While she settled on the padded seat, he grabbed the other chair and placed it in front of her before he sat.

The soothing sounds of birds singing calmed her racing heart until his knees touched her. He was so close. Heat filled her. How would she cope if she was already going up in flames? Now she knew why her ex left her feeling colder than a dead fish.

Becca shook her head. No thinking about her ex. This was about her and Tyler.

"You're nervous."

Damn. The man could already read her. She bit her lower lip before nodding.

He studied her. "Why?"

She swallowed. "I've never done anything like this be-fore."

"Becca." He took her hands in his, thumbs brushing the backs of her knuckles in a soothing motion.

Or would have been soothing if her nerves weren't jumping under her skin.

"We're only going to talk. We haven't seen each other in a long time, and we need to get re-acquainted. We also need to discuss what you want to do here at the ranch."

"You're not going to tell me?"

"I'll guide you, yes. It's your decision on what you do or don't do."

Her teeth worried her bottom lip. *This is what I wanted, right?*

Maybe? She also wanted a man who would give her sensual pleasure. This—the control being hers— wasn't what she expected at all. "I think I'm a little confused."

"I can imagine. Let's get some of the basics out of the way. I'm healthy and STI-free. I can provide you with my latest test results, if you want."

Oh, Lord, I didn't even think about that. "I recently tested negative too." She'd had her annual physical a few weeks back, and since she hadn't had sex in over two years, she wasn't worried.

"Are you on the pill?"

Becca shifted in her seat. She better get used to frank discussions. "I am."

"Good." He squeezed her hands. "I'll use a condom until you feel comfortable."

Her breath caught. In college, they'd always used a condom. But the image of him being bare as they made love made her pussy pulse.

"I know what kind of sex you used to enjoy, but what do you like now?"

"Huh?" She tilted her head to the side, staring at him. "I don't know what you mean?"

His chuckle floated in the air between them. "Did you read the activities book about the ranch? What do you want to try?"

"Ahh." She squirmed. How could she talk about this? How could she not?

"We're consenting adults," he continued. "Nothing is taboo here. Anything you want. If it's legal, I'll do my best to provide, or find someone who will."

"Someone who will..." Her voice trailed off.

"Only if you want."

Becca swallowed. The ball was back in her court. She wanted Tyler. Okay, that was pretty obvious, but why was this discussion so difficult? She never had trouble talking sex with Angie.

Angie wasn't Tyler, though. He was a living, breathing, sex-on-two legs, fully-grown male. Her gaze slid over his body. She knew what he was packing in his jeans.

"Let it go, Becca."

"What?"

"Your embarrassment, inhibitions, whatever is stopping you from talking to me. We were lovers. No judgment here."

"I don't know what's holding me back. I don't know what the hell I want."

He grinned, and while she wanted to be annoyed with him, she knew her confusion wasn't his fault.

"I see." He released her hands, and she missed his warmth. Pushing the chair back, he rubbed the back of his neck. "Do you trust me?"

"Yes." The admission surprised her.

"That was a quick answer. I've changed from the guy you knew in college."

They hadn't seen each other in years, but in the past, he'd been a gentle, generous lover. Her trust in him was still there; otherwise, she wouldn't have agreed to be his partner.

"I've changed too." She'd buried the wild and carefree girl she'd been when she became a responsible woman.

That wasn't a bad thing, but she was tired of being responsible.

"I can see that. Bet you've been suppressing your sexuality."

His insight startled her. "What makes you say that?"

"Down by the stables, you were tense. You think I can't remember the signs? You couldn't relax at dinner. My Becca was more outgoing and talked with people all the time."

Becca nodded. He wasn't wrong.

"You never thought twice about touching someone in support, be it a pat on the back or a quick hug. The woman in front of me seems closed down, suppressing the vibrant side of herself."

While she wanted to deny it, she couldn't. Yet another reason to have this carefree week and let herself go. Her new job would be as stressful as her last one, but it was her dream job. She'd need all her wits about her for that, so why not relax while she could.

"So, what are you going to do about it?" The words slipped from her before she could censor them.

"Free her," he whispered. "Everything we do will be with consent. If there is something you don't want to do, you'll have a safe word. You say that, and everything stops."

She frowned. "Does that mean I have to leave? If I use my safe word?"

He shook his head. "It means we stop and discuss why you used it. It's perfectly fine to safeword if you feel unsafe or unsure of what we're doing. We will discuss it and then decide to try again or skip it."

She liked that. "All right. I consent to whatever you feel is best." It was a leap of faith, but one she needed to make.

"Tomorrow, you will attend the lecture called *Revitalizing Your Sex Life with Communication.*"

"Somehow, I don't think my sex life needs revitalizing. It's alive and kicking right now." She punctuated her words with laughter. Oh, yes, her body was reacting in ways it hadn't in years.

He grinned. "There's more to the lecture than you know. It will help you open up, to communicate with your partner. I want you to be honest with me no matter what."

Maybe Tyler was right. Communication hadn't been forefront in her past relationships.

"Tell me what you want to try." When she didn't speak, he trailed his fingers over her cheek, leaving a path of heat. "No fear, no embarrassment."

Becca took a breath and blew it out. *Why is this so hard?* Glancing over his shoulder, her gaze focused on one of the privacy bushes. Maybe if she didn't look at him, she'd be able to tell him what she wanted.

"Ummmm...toys."

"What else?"

Tension crept into her body. "Bondage."

"There's a wide spectrum with bondage from light to hardcore."

"Light."

"Got it. Next?"

She closed her eyes. "Anal." Everything inside her froze as she spoke the word. She didn't want to see his reaction, afraid he'd think her abnormal, as past lovers had.

His hand closed over hers and he squeezed. "Look at me, please."

She finally opened her eyes. There was no shock or disgust in his features, only acceptance and a flare of excitement.

"No problem there." He tilted his head just the slightest bit. "But there's more, isn't there?"

Her gaze left his face as she stood and pulled her hand away, then moved to the edge of the patio. She paced back to Tyler, turned without speaking, and paced to the edge again. Would Tyler understand her fantasy of adding another lover to the mix? Just once, she wanted to experience two men loving her. She wasn't sure she could voice the deep dark desire within her.

Her fingers curled into her palms as she paced the small enclosure. Tyler's scent of pine and masculinity made it hard to think. His hands on her shoulders stopped her pacing, and she turned and glanced up at him.

"I won't judge you."

"You wouldn't be a co-owner here if you judged people based on their sexual preferences."

"Tell me." His voice had dropped a notch.

Her muscles tightened, and her belly clenched until she thought she was going to scream, but she couldn't voice her desire. She shook her head.

"Do you want to experiment with another woman?"

She shook her head.

"Another man?"

She felt herself flinch in his grasp. He was guessing, but it was more than experimenting with another man.

"Is that it?" His head lowered. "Do you want two men pleasuring you? To worship your body, to take you to heights you've only dreamed about?"

She sagged in his hold. "Yes."

"My Becca." His lips brushed her cheek. "I think we'll have a marvelous time together."

"What if..." She bit her lower lip.

"What if what?"

Taking a deep breath, she forced the words out. "What if I can't do something you expect?" There, she said it. Yes, they'd been lovers, but they'd both changed. Plus, for the past eight years, she hadn't lived up to anyone's expectations. Hell, not even her own.

"My expectations?" She heard disbelief in his tone. The next thing she knew, he gently caught her chin and tipped her face toward his. "I do not expect anything from you. This is all *for* you, Becca. This is a safe place for you to explore your sexuality and sensuality. *My* expectations have no place here."

The sincerity in his voice and his expression alleviated her concern. "But what if I can't do something I've said I want to try?"

"Not an issue. Communication at all times between us. If we try something and you don't like it, we will stop."

"You won't force me?"

"Consent is important. I might push you out of your comfort zone, but I would never force you." He lowered his forehead until it touched hers. "Remember we will have a safe word, and the second you use it, I will stop. This is about pleasure, not pain. Your pleasure, Becca, not mine."

She met his gaze head on, and hooked her fingers in his belt loops. "Then let's do it." It was time to let go of everything. She had this one week. Becca felt the stress and tension leave her body.

"Why don't we go for a horseback ride?"

She smiled. "I'd like that."

This week was going to be so much fun.

Chapter Six

♥

Tyler kept an eye on Becca as he saddled his stallion. She was eyeing the horse and he understood. Thunder was a big horse, but gentle as a gelding. Which was a good thing since they were riding tandem and she was a total novice rider.

All that talk about expectations... What man would expect a woman to do something she wasn't comfortable with? An insecure one or an idiot. *I hope she's not still worrying about me forcing her into anything.* He'd make sure to reinforce that she was in control.

Becca was perfect the way she was. Even in college, she'd been a willing and open lover. Admittedly, their sex wasn't too adventurous, mainly different positions, him pinning her arms over her head, a little playful spanking.

But nothing like what they were going to do here.

He'd learned a lot over the years they'd been apart, and the anticipation of exploration excited him.

Becca shifted from one foot to the other. Was she nervous? Or aroused? Probably a bit of both. "Since we don't have time for a full riding lesson today, we're going to ride tandem."

"What's that?" she asked.

He smiled. "We'll ride the same horse."

Her cheeks turned pink.

"I know a place where we can sit and talk."

"Haven't we talked enough?" Her exasperation made him chuckle.

"That's usually a man's response, but no, we haven't." He motioned her over to him. Once she was by his side, he maneuvered her into position. "Put your left foot into the stirrup."

He waited while she complied.

"When I say lift, push yourself up and, throw your right leg over the saddle. Don't worry, I'll help you."

"Sure. Sounds easy." There was a note of doubt in her voice.

"One, two, three, *up*." Damn, she was light. He'd observed this yesterday, but today it seemed even more evident. He would make sure she ate well while she was here.

He smiled to himself. *She'll need her energy for what I have planned.*

"Great job," he said as she shifted in the saddle. He slid her foot from the stirrup, and she made a little cry. "Easy." He gripped her leg. "I need the stirrup to climb up behind you."

He mounted behind her in one quick motion. Her fingers clenched the saddle horn when the horse shifted beneath them. "It's okay," he said, lifting the reins.

"Are you talking to me or the horse?" Her voice sounded unsteady.

"Both." He adjusted in the saddle. Because many couples liked riding double, they had custom-made saddles that would fit two people comfortably, and several horses sturdy enough to carry two people.

Becca's ass rubbed against his groin, and his cock jumped. Tyler closed his eyes and fought for self-control, something that had never been an issue before. His arms tightened around Becca.

"Is this a good idea?"

"The best." Maybe the best torture. "Lean back against me." Her back felt warm against his chest. He wanted to hold her, touch her, make her come screaming his name. Now was not the time for that. Soon, though. Very soon.

Tyler clicked his tongue, and Becca made a noise and stiffened when the horse began to walk. He moved so that his lips barely brushed her ear, glad her hair was up. Maybe later, he'd let it down.

"I won't let you fall," he whispered. "Feel the horse beneath you, the way he moves, and allow your body to sway with him in a delicate dance."

Her ass wiggled as she tried to follow the horse's gait. His cock was happy dancing within his jeans, hoping to be released so it could sink into Becca's warm pussy.

Not now. Anticipation was part of the game. Based on what she'd told him, he was already working out a schedule in his mind for what classes she would attend.

How surprised would she be when she attended the toy lecture and found out he was the instructor? He already knew what toys he wanted to use to make her skin flush, to tantalize, to arouse, to make her come, and to make her scream with pleasure. He turned the horse toward the trail.

"It's beautiful out here," she said, bringing him back to the present.

"Yes." The horse knew the trail well and followed it with little direction from him, which was a good thing since all he could concentrate on was Becca. "Jared and I bought the land a little over five years ago."

"Why an adult ranch?"

"It didn't start out that way." He nudged the horse to take the right trail at the fork so they would enter a more heavily wooded area of the ranch. "We originally planned a normal dude ranch, until Jared attended a conference in San Francisco."

"What kind of conference?" Her body now moved with the horse as she relaxed.

Oh boy, how will she react to this?

He cleared his throat. "A therapy conference."

"As in physical therapy?"

"No. Jared is a licensed sexual psychologist."

"Oh. That's... interesting."

He smiled. Everyone reacted differently to hearing about Jared's specialty. "At the conference, Jared realized there was no place for couples to explore their sexual side. When he returned to the ranch, he proposed the idea."

"Aren't there clubs or such for people to explore their kinky side?"

"There are, but we wanted something more intimate."

"I have a feeling you took to it like a surfer to water."

His tension eased at her playful tone. "Naturally. Do you remember my major at State?"

"Partying," she said without hesitation.

Tyler chuckled. "You aren't wrong there." He did like to party and that was how he met Becca. "My other major was human development."

"That's right. Human development with a heavy dose of sex thrown into the mix."

Her banter made him realize how much he missed companionship with a woman who both challenged him and wouldn't take him to task about his job, his life, or his sexuality.

"Hey, I like sex, and you do too. Right?"

"Nothing wrong with that." Her butt wiggled against his hard cock.

"Behave, or you might get a ride on my horse you weren't expecting."

She gasped and stilled. "Continue with your story."

It took Tyler a minute to remember what they were talking about. "We decided to create a place where consenting adults could explore their sexuality in a safe environment. It took us almost two years to build the place and hire the right people. Plus, we had to be careful how we advertised."

"You don't want the locals or the police interfering with your business."

"Partially, but we didn't want people to think they were coming here just for sex. We have all the proper permits.

Quick Silver Ranch is a place to explore and discover, not just to fuck your brains out."

"Oh, darn. I was looking forward to fucking like bunnies."

Her laughter made him grin. "For you, I'll make an exception." Hell, he'd do anything for Becca. The thought should scare him, but he realized how closed off he'd been in the last year. "Advertising wasn't really something we had to worry about. With Jared's connections in the psychology community, we had couples lining up. Word of mouth really does sell the product."

"One of the couples last night said they'd been here before."

"Yes. Repeat visitors are common. Gives people a chance to get away from the pressure of their lives, but also the freedom to explore sexual practices that some might consider taboo."

"Like anal sex."

"Yes, or a ménage, or some might even consider bondage unnatural. Here, we give the couples the freedom to try anything they want. We also give them instructions on how to be safe doing so."

Tilting her head back, she glanced at him. "What happened to your degree in animal science that you went to Humboldt for?"

"I have that too. A degree in animal husbandry along with a degree in human development. I manage the horses and the grounds personnel; Jared manages the hospitality staff."

Tyler guided the horse onto the smaller path, then into the clearing, where he brought them to a stop. Dismounting, he grimaced at the tightness of his jeans.

He reached up and put his hands on Becca's waist. "Swing your leg over and slide down. I've got you."

She followed his instructions, and he held her close when her feet touched the ground. He had her right where he wanted her—in his arms, against his body, and he wanted to lay her down here in this quiet meadow, strip her bare, and bury his dick inside her pussy.

The air brushing their naked skin, the sky filled with the cries of her passion.

Hold on, buddy. There was a lot of ground they needed to cover before he could even begin to think about having sex with Becca.

"Okay?" He needed to put some space between them before he lost all his good intentions. Not that he had any. One week. He only had one week with Becca. How serious could things get in a week?

"I'm fine." She stepped out of his hold.

"Good." He removed the leather hobble from the horse's neck and gave him a good scritch behind the left ear before he secured the hobble below the knees of his front legs. After a gentle stroke from forehead to muzzle, he opened the saddlebags. He pulled out a blanket and a couple of small pillows. Tucking them under his arm, he captured her hand.

He scanned the area and determined the best place for them to sit—near the rocks that would serve as a nice backrest. He released her hand and dropped the pillows, then spread the blanket.

"Have a seat." Tyler waved his hand.

She lowered herself onto the blanket, and Tyler slid to his knees. He reached up and brushed stray hair away from her face.

Becca flinched at his touch.

"Touching is an integral part of this week." He skimmed his fingers over her hair and found the pins at the back of her head. He removed them.

Hair as soft as pure silk flowed over his hand when he removed the last of the pins. He resisted the urge to bury his face in its waves and inhale what he was sure was her unique fragrance. All woman.

"I know." He smiled at the note of exasperation in her response. Probably from being sexually frustrated.

"You may not know it, but you're far from relaxed. What is it? On the horse, you were bantering with me, wiggling against me. What's changed?"

"I…" Her hand fluttered to her throat.

He didn't have a clue why she was so nervous. Maybe he could make this a bit more pleasant for her.

"Let's try this." Maneuvering his body, he picked up a pillow and placed it against the rock. He sat back into the natural depression. "Come here." He spread his legs and patted the ground between his thighs.

Becca stared at him but she slid between his thighs. Once again, her butt rested against his groin, her back against his chest, and her head resting on his shoulder. There was still tension in her body.

"That's better." He settled his arms around her waist but kept his touch light. "How much sexual experience have you had since we were together?"

"I could ask you the same thing."

He chuckled. There was the fire he was looking for. "I haven't been a monk, but I'm not the hound dog you seem to think I am. It's been a while since I've had a lover." Not since nine months ago, when his fiancée decided her job was more important than he was.

"It's been over two years for me."

He sucked in a breath. "By choice?"

She tensed. "Not really." She sighed and melted against him. "My ex had some issues and didn't want to sleep with me before the wedding. Even so, we did come close one time, and he found my BOB and freaked out."

"BOB?"

"Battery-Operated Boyfriend."

Laughter spilled from Tyler. He couldn't help it. "The man was an insecure idiot."

"To say the least."

"You said ex. What happened?" How bad had this man hurt her? And he wasn't the one who tried to force her, if he freaked out over a vibrator.

"A few days ago, I found him in bed with my boss. Or should I say ex-boss. When I discovered them together, I broke off my engagement. And I quit my job but, thankfully, I already have a new job lined up. I'll be head of catering at a large hotel."

Her words set off mini bombs inside Tyler. How could any man cheat on her? Let alone not fuck her? *Wait a minute.* Trips to the ranch had to be booked months in advance, so that meant she was supposed to be here with the ex.

"If he was upset about the vibrator, why were the two of you coming here?"

"My best friend, Angie, purchased this visit as pre-wedding trip. She probably figured Alan would loosen up once we were here. She couldn't have been more wrong. Alan didn't want *me*, so this trip wouldn't have made a bit of difference." Her palms curved over the back of his hands where they rested on her belly.

"But you're here alone?"

"Angie encouraged me to get away for the week. I was between jobs, and I didn't want to be home if Alan came around trying to make excuses, so why not get away?"

"I'm glad you did." He nudged her hair out of the way with his nose and gently blew in her ear, delighted when she shivered.

"I am too. That's why I know I'm not on the rebound, because Alan wasn't the right man for me. I knew that deep down, or I wouldn't have been so damn calm when I caught him in bed with another man."

"What the fuck!" The words were out of Tyler's mouth before he could stop them.

"Yep. Surprised me too. But it explained why he didn't want to have sex with me."

Stunned, Tyler's mind struggled to play catch-up when Becca shifted position and pulled him back to the present.

That was enough about the ex. "Would you like to hear what I have planned for the week?" He wanted her relaxed, and talking about the week would help.

"Yes, please."

"Tomorrow, you'll go to the *Revitalizing Your Sex Life with Communication* lecture. This is the only lecture I won't be attending with you. The lecture will take up your morning, and afterward, I'll meet you at your cabin for lunch." Her swift intake of breath had him wondering what she was thinking.

"And what will we do in the afternoon?" she softly asked.

"Go over what you've learned. And other things."

She relaxed once again. A good sign. "And the next day?."

"Toy lecture." He didn't mention he was teaching that particular class. He wanted her to be surprised.

"I know about toys."

"Is BOB your only experience with toys?"

"Yes."

"There's a lot more to learn. The lecture is in the morning, then in the afternoon we'll review what you've learned and put things into practice."

"I like the sound of that." Her voice almost had a drowsy quality to it. She turned her head on his shoulder and smiled at him before kissing his chin.

His cock thickened, and her eyes lit up. He knew she felt his cock against her ass. *Let's see if...* He shifted, rotating his hips.

"Feels good." She pressed her ass against him, and if he wasn't careful, he'd lose control. For moment, he almost said the hell with it but pulled himself back. "The next day will be the anal lecture."

Her eyes closed, concealing her gaze from him, but her breathing increased.

"Then bondage. And Friday, your last class will be on ménages."

Her cheeks filled with color. "You'll be with me in all the classes but the first one, right?"

"Yes."

"Good." She sighed, and the tension left her body as she rested against him, her hands settled against her sides.

"Tell me what you like." He stroked her belly with light strokes through her clothing.

"Like?"

"Sexually. What turns you on? What makes you so hot you can't wait to tear the clothes off your partner and have your wicked way with him?"

"What about you?"

Interesting. Every time she became uncomfortable, she tried to deflect by throwing the question back at him. "This is about you, not me."

A puff of breath brushed over his skin. "I'm not sure what turns me on."

What the hell? He almost blurted it out. The Becca he knew hadn't been shy about telling him what turned her on. What else had changed in the last eight years?

"Are you aroused sitting here with my cock pressing against your ass?"

"Yes."

"What about this?" He cupped her right breast and massaged it. Her nipple hardened beneath the fabric.

"Oh yes." Her voice sounded softer and her breathing faster.

"And this?" His left hand slipped down, tracking the seam of her jeans over her pussy. Even through the denim her heat came through.

"Oh god, yes." She shifted her hips.

"Not yet, sweetheart." He ached to lower the zipper on her jeans and plunge his fingers into her moistness, but he would wait. Today was for them to get reacquainted, for him to find out about her sexual experience or lack thereof.

"Tease."

"I'm going to tease you without mercy this week." His lips brushed against her temple. He would need all his patience to get through this.

***

Becca shifted closer to Tyler. Well, as much as she could. She wanted him. But it was more than just want and need.

Why am I hesitating? They'd been lovers, but she was aware they were different people than they had been eight years ago. Only Tyler could so easily bring out her sensual side. She needed to allow herself to explore and not think about the past.

His arms were around her waist, and his brief touches fueled the need in her body. Turning her head, she pressed her lips against his. For a minute, she thought he might stop her, then his arms tightened around her.

His tongue traced the seam of her lips, and she opened to him. He teased her, dipping in and out of her mouth. She wanted to deepen the kiss, but the way he held her made it impossible. Instead, she lifted her arm and curled it around his neck, urging him to kiss her deeper, harder.

A moan escaped her when he broke the kiss off. "Talk to me. I want to know what you're feeling."

Ugh. Her mother taught her from earliest childhood not to reveal emotion. Even after Becca moved out and away from her mother, she still had trouble expressing her feelings to anyone.

"I don't know if I can." Her arm fell from around his neck into her lap, her fingers curling into her palms.

His hold on her waist tightened, then loosened. His right hand covered her breast. "What am I doing?"

"Caressing my breast."

"What does it feel like?"

She wrinkled her nose. "Good."

"I know you can do better than that, sweetheart." When she didn't answer, he continued. "Close your eyes and rest your head on my shoulder again. Talk to me, don't censor yourself. There's nothing you can say that will make me walk away from you."

Becca wasn't sure about that. She took a deep breath, laid her head back on his shoulder, and closed her eyes. She let her mind empty of all her negative thoughts and concentrated on Tyler's hand on her breast, his arm around her waist, his breath against her skin.

Oh, my... Her nerves were alive and moving under her skin, coming alive and enjoying his touch. She hadn't felt like this since...Tyler in college. "Your caress is tender, not too hard, but not too soft." Shivers of excitement tingled along her spine. It had been so long. "Ohhhh." The noise escaped her when he pinched her nipple. A surge of arousal hit her.

His lips brushed her temple. "If something I do hurts, or you don't like it, let me know."

"Okay." She squirmed against him when he cupped left breast with his other hand. Lightning coursed through her body as he caressed, plucked, and played with her nipples. She wanted more. She wanted his bare skin against hers.

"Touch me," she begged.

"I am."

"No." She shook her head trying to find the words. "Really touch me. I want your hands on my bare skin. I want to feel your fingers pinch my nipples." Heat spread as she spoke. This was unexpected but welcome.

"Your wish is my command." He slid his hands from her breasts to her abdomen and pushed up the hem of her shirt. "Lean forward for me, sweetheart."

She did as he asked, and at the same time realized she usually objected to anyone calling her sweetheart.

But coming from Tyler, she liked it. He said it in a soft, sexy voice that made her toes curl. He slid her shirt up and over her head, discarding it on the blanket.

His fingers trailed up her spine, tracing a light path until he found the hooks on her bra. With deft movements, he released the hooks, and the bra joined her shirt on the blanket. The soft fabric of his shirt caressed her back as he settled her against his body.

His hands stilled against her belly. "Better?"

"Yes. The air is dancing over my skin." Now that the words flowed from her, she wouldn't stop them. "My nipples are getting hard, begging for your touch."

"I see." He traced her areola with the pad of his finger, sending heat coursing through her body. "You have beautiful breasts. So full, and your nipples… I can't wait to put clamps on them."

A zing of arousal flowed to her pussy, and moisture collected in her panties. "Clamps?" Why did the thought excite her?

"Would you like that?" He teased her with the tip of his nail, lightly scraping across her taut nipple.

"I'm not sure."

Angie dragged her into an adult store once. There, Becca saw nipple clamps, but they looked more like torture devices than something for pleasure. She had tried out a set of nipple rings, and liked the feeling of them…

Until her then-boyfriend saw them and freaked out.

Tyler tweaked her nipple, bringing her attention back to the present. "You're thinking too hard."

"How did you know that?" Could she not keep a single secret from him?

"You tensed. What were you thinking about?"

Becca bit her lower lip. "My best friend, Angie, took me to an adult shop once."

"When was that?"

"About four years ago. I bought a pair of nipple rings."

"Did you wear them?"

"Yes. They were adjustable, sort of like a ring. I could squeeze them just enough they stayed on." She shifted. Thinking about those rings was making her body ache.

"Did you like them?"

"They excited me, and I enjoyed them, until…" She shivered at the memory.

"Until what? What happened?"

"The man I was dating at the time saw them and called me depraved."

"Asshole." Tyler widened his touch to include her breasts and not just her nipple. "Nipple rings are a nice enhancement to what nature provided you. And since you've used them, clamps will be easier." His lips touched her ear. "Think about having clamps on these hard buds." His voice dropped to a husky whisper.

Her belly somersaulted with excitement at his words. He tweaked her nipples, and pure pleasure flowed through her as her breath caught in her throat. If he could do this with his touch, what would happen if they made love?

Wait, I'm getting ahead of myself. While they were at an adult ranch and sex was on the table, it wouldn't happen that fast.

Would it?

"With my clamps, there's a small chain between them. It will hang down so I can tug it at will. And I will tug it as I lick your pussy until you come all over my mouth. Then I'll do it again and again until you're screaming with the pleasure only I can give you."

Oh. Dear. God! His words, along with him tugging at her nipples, hyper focused her on the sensations coursing from her nipples all the way to her toes. Her clit pulsed with need at the feel of his hard cock pressed against her ass. His lips caressed her ear, and she moaned.

"Would you like that, sweetheart?"

"Fuck yes," she breathed. She turned her head enough so she could capture his lips with hers. She needed to taste him. Their tongues tangled and dueled before parting, only to merge again.

All the while, he played with her nipples, and she rubbed her ass against his hard dick. Her panties were soaked, and she didn't care. She wanted, no, *needed* more.

Tearing her mouth away, she said, "I want to touch you." Was that her breathless voice?

His blue eyes darkened with desire before he dropped a soft kiss against her lips, and his mouth trailed up to her temple. "Later," he whispered, one hand trailing from her breasts to the top of her jeans. "Unzip them for me."

She fumbled with the button because her hand trembled. It finally came loose, and she lowered the zipper.

"Are you wet?"

Her gut clenched when his palm slid beneath her panties.

"You are." His fingers slid between her pussy lips, stroking her ever so lightly.

"Tyler." She shifted her hips, trying to get his fingers deeper or at least to touch her clit.

"What do you want?"

"You." She sighed as he pressed a finger into her. "Please." She was begging. It had been too long since a man aroused her this much.

"So soft. So wet." Her clothing restricted his movements a bit, but he still managed to slip a second finger in. "I can feel you tightening around my fingers."

"Feels so good." It did, and she wanted it to last. "Too long. I—" An orgasm unexpectedly tore through her.

"That's it, baby, let it go. Come for me. Let me feel your passion, your pleasure."

His words fueled her pleasure as her body shuddered around his fingers. Her breathing was erratic even after her climax subsided, and she sagged against his body.

She panted out her next words. "I want you inside me."

But he didn't answer. Instead, he withdrew his fingers from her pulsing core, zipped, and fastened her jeans. Next, he urged her to sit up as he picked up her bra.

"Tyler? Why are you dressing me?"

"This is about anticipation." He slipped her bra on and fastened it, followed by her shirt.

Becca shook her head. "To hell with anticipation!" But Tyler had already slipped out from behind her and was standing, and holding a hand out to her.

"I..." He pulled her to her feet and pressed his finger against her lips. She was about to protest when she heard the rustling of leaves and voices. Someone else was here. Is that why Tyler stopped?

He nudged her in the direction of the bushes, and she saw Peter and Maggie through the tall brush in another clearing. She remembered them from dinner. She didn't notice a horse anywhere, they must have hiked out here.

They'd spread two blankets in the small clearing, and the couple laid naked, caressing each other. Becca averted her eyes. "We should go," she whispered.

"Haven't you ever wanted to watch another couple?" His voice was playful.

Swallowing hard, she kept her gaze on Tyler's face. She'd never thought of herself as a voyeur, but the idea excited her.

"Yes, that's it, baby." Maggie's voice carried through the air. "I want that big boy to fill me on the first thrust. Take me. Fill me with your come and don't stop until I'm screaming."

"I can't," she hissed. "They don't even know we're here. I feel like we're violating consent."

"Are you sure?"

"Yes, please. This isn't fair to them." A duet of groans reached them.

Tyler slid his arms around her waist and slowly backed them away. "How would you like to have another person or couple watch us as I fuck you?" Tyler's husky words sent a shiver of exhilaration through her bloodstream. "Their eyes on your body with your nipples hard and begging to be touched, my cock plunging in and out of your wet pussy. And they're watching everything, every move, every stroke, knowing you're *mine*."

Her knees grew weak, and she barely held back a moan.

"Just think about it." His arms disappeared, and she swayed for a moment before she found her balance. Tyler picked up the blanket and pillows in their area. He put them away before taking her hand and Thunder's reins, and they walked away, putting space between them and the couple before mounting the horse.

It was bad enough she was aroused by Tyler, but the other couple's words had stoked that fire even higher. The flames licked against her skin as Tyler's cock pressed against her ass while they rode back to the stable.

What would happen if they were both naked on the back of the horse? If she leaned forward and reached back, could she direct his cock into her pussy? How would it feel to have him pumping in and out of her in time with the horse's movement? Would he have the horse run so he could fuck her fast and hard or walk and make it slow and torturous?

Her body was burning up. At this rate, she was not only going to need a very cold shower, but a vibrator. Except she hadn't packed one. Hell, this was an adult ranch. There had to be one she could buy and use.

"Your skin is flushed and your breathing is choppy. What are you thinking about?"

"You, me, naked on this horse." The words came out before she could stop them.

"I take it you're picturing us fucking?"

"Yes." Becca swallowed, her head resting against Tyler's shoulder, as she tried to control her thoughts. By the time they arrived at the stables, her body was on fire. She was so aroused the fabric of her bra irritated her nipples.

Tyler helped her down from the horse, and she clung to him. "Tyler."

"Later, Becca." He brushed a kiss over her lips.

"But—"

"I need to take care of the horse, and we both need to cool down. I'll see you at dinner."

He winked, turned, and led the horse away. Becca was about to call out to him when she noticed him reach around... *Did he adjust himself?* He was suffering as much as she was. But for some reason didn't want to act on his desire.

So why is he waiting? Tyler must have his reasons. Not that she liked it, but she would accept it.

Without saying a word, she turned and made her way to her cabin. A cold shower would help cool her down, but only another good orgasm would calm her down. She hadn't felt this aroused since college.

Since Tyler.

Chapter Seven

♥

Tyler watched Becca's hips sway with each step as she walked away from the barn, his cock pulsing in time with her motion. The woman oozed sex, and this was only the beginning. She was going to test his control to the limits.

He led Thunder into the stables, working on autopilot as he tended to the horse before making his way to the main house. Jogging up the stairs, he headed to his private rooms, stripped, and stepped into the shower.

The cold water made him grit his teeth when it flowed his overheated skin, and it wasn't all from the horse grooming. He braced his arms against the tile wall, letting the water sluice over his body, willing his dick to soften.

It didn't.

Shivering, he growled in frustration, turned the water warmer, and scrubbed his skin so he wouldn't show up to dinner smelling of horse. Finishing up, he dried off and strode into his bedroom.

His cock slapped against his skin with each step. The damn thing had a mind of its own, and right now, it wanted Becca. Waiting sucked, but it was the right thing to do. Flopping down on his bed, he reached over and opened the nightstand drawer. He pulled out a condom and one of his favorite toys.

After slipping the condom on, he placed the sleeve over his sheathed cock. Settling against the pillows, he took the bulb in his hand and began squeezing. Fuck, his hips rose with the first pump. He was on edge. Closing his eyes, he thought about how Becca would look in the clearing as they made love, her long brown hair spread over the blanket, her breasts swollen, her nipples hard from his mouth and fingers, her pussy wet when he caressed her clit.

He pumped the bulb fast while he fantasized about encasing her hard nubs in clamps, the silver chain dangling between her ripe breasts as she straddled him, her head facing his feet and his dick pointed at her mouth.

Oh, yeah. The chain would dangle against his abs as she went down on him. He couldn't help but tug on it. She'd pull him deep into her mouth, sucking him. He'd pull the chain harder watching her body flush. Her pussy glistening above him, his tongue would swipe the moisture gathered there.

As his balls tightened, he squeezed the bulb in his hand harder, consumed by his fantasy. His fingers parted those rosy pussy lips before plunging two fingers into her. Becca would moan as he leaned up and captured her clit with his mouth.

Within minutes, she would be screaming in pleasure...

And that's when his cock exploded. His hips arched higher as his climax hit him hard. But he didn't stop squeezing the bulb, pretending it was Becca's mouth, until he was sure his balls were empty.

Tyler slumped against the mattress, his body covered in a fine sweat. Damn, now he needed another shower, but he didn't care. His cock was satisfied, the man not as much. He wanted Becca in his arms. He couldn't wait for tomorrow. Once Becca's lessons started, she wouldn't know what hit her.

With a groan, he removed the toy and walked back into his bathroom. Tomorrow was a new day.

***

Becca woke to music. Music? She shook her head and then remembered she'd left the MP3 player on repeat last night since she didn't have her phone. The cabin had been too quiet, and she couldn't stand it.

Throwing the covers aside, she slid out of bed. The cool air flowed over her naked body. She never slept in the nude.

This was Tyler's fault. After their ride, she'd returned to her cabin and masturbated. Her body was satisfied until dinner, when Tyler sat next to her, his masculine scent teasing her.

It didn't help that he touched her every chance he got, making it clear that they were partners now. Her body was so sensitive to him. When he'd glanced her way with those blazing blue eyes, her pussy flooded. Throughout dinner she fought the urge to grab him, strip him, and fuck him on the dining room table, not caring who watched.

That scared her. She'd never reacted to a man like this, not even when she and Tyler were together in college. Yes, he'd been insatiable—both of them were—but nothing like this.

After dinner he walked her back to her cabin and left her on the doorstep with another deep scorching, wet kiss before telling her he'd see her in the morning. He even had the nerve to whistle as he left. She stomped into the cabin and immediately searched for a vibrator.

The freestanding cabinet in the bedroom was pad-locked, and she couldn't find a key anywhere in the cabin.

Why would an adult ranch lock up their vibrators? She could call and ask about obtaining a vibrator, but that would be embarrassing, especially if Tyler answered the phone.

Instead, she used her fingers but still went to bed frustrated and needy.

Becca glanced at the clock next to the bed. Damn, eight. She'd better get a move on if she was going to shower, dress, and eat before her first lecture at ten.

After grabbing clothes out of the dresser, she took a quick shower. Her body was sweaty from her erotic dreams last night. At this rate, with as many showers as she was taking, she'd need to bathe in lotion so her skin wouldn't dry out. Once dressed, she headed to the ranch house to grab coffee and breakfast. At nine fifty-five, Becca walked into the lecture building.

She found the right room and walked in. Maggie and Sally were already there.

"Hi, Becca," they chorused.

"Hi." She bit her lip and was about to take a seat when a perky blonde woman all but bounced into the room.

"Hi, ladies. I'm Liza, and I'll be your instructor today. Since we're a small group, why don't we sit on the mats and get comfortable?"

Becca followed the other women to the front of the room and lowered herself onto the gray mat. They sat in a loosely formed circle.

"That's better," Liza said. "We'll start off with introductions, then on to the lecture. I've been on staff here since the ranch opened, as has most of the staff. I'm married to Bart, who is another instructor. I'm also one of the housekeepers." Liza paused and looked at each of them. "Tell me why you're in this lecture. Maggie, why don't you start?"

"I wanted to see how communication can spice up my love life."

"Me, too, plus exploring the more exotic side of sex," Sally chimed in.

All gazes turned to her. "Ummm. Tyler recommended the class." What else could she say? Becca took a deep breath. "My best friend gave me this trip as a pre-wedding present, I was supposed to be here with my fiancé, but I found him in bed with my boss six days ago." Six days? It seemed like a lifetime ago.

"Bastard," Sally said.

"You're better off without him," Maggie commented.

Becca smiled her thanks to the women. "My friend convinced me to take this trip anyway. I didn't know it was an adult ranch for couples."

Liza nodded. "Interesting that Tyler volunteered to be your partner."

Becca bit her lip, then figured it wouldn't hurt to tell them. "Not so far-fetched. Tyler and I went to college together. We were lovers back then."

Liza grinned. "Now that makes sense. Thank you for sharing. This lecture concentrates on communication with your partner. We know there are a lot of lectures to take in, and it's fine to be here without your partner. We encourage you to split up when possible and then report back to each other."

"Charlie wanted to come with me," Sally said. "But I sent him to the cunnilingus class. He needs help in that direction."

"I sent Peter to the sexual positions class," Maggie added. "Sometimes he forgets missionary can be a bit boring."

Everyone laughed, and Becca's tension began to ease.

"You both communicated with your partners on what you'd prefer, and that's what this class is about," Liza said. "How to communicate your fantasies and desires to your partner."

Fantasies? Becca tilted her head. This would be very interesting.

"The first step is to forget all your inhibitions; they don't belong here. And forget anything else you've been conditioned to think about sex and fantasies. Noting is taboo at Quick Silver Ranch. Today, you are free. Sally, tell us a fantasy. If you could do anything you wanted with Charlie, what would it be?"

Becca swallowed. *What the heck will I say when it's my turn?* She forced herself to concentrate on what Sally was saying. Maybe she could pick up some pointers.

***

Tyler knocked on Becca's cabin door right before one. He'd worked like a demon last night and this morning to make sure he had the afternoon free to spend with Becca. Yes, he could have delegated a lot of his jobs, but he'd need his workers' help later in the week.

He'd stopped to talk with Liza to find out, asking her how the morning workshop went. All she told him was he was lucky to have a partner like Becca.

So where is she? He knocked again, harder. No answer.

He pursed his lips in frustration. This time, he knocked even harder and called out her name. He could use the master key, and he would if she didn't answer this time.

"Just a second." A muffled voice yelled. She flung the door open a minute later.

Becca's face looked flushed, her hair half in and half out of a ponytail. Her breathing was erratic, and her nipples stood hard against the fabric of her T-shirt. Did she forget their meeting?

His gaze traveled over her body. A pair of short-shorts and bare feet. She shifted from one foot to the other as his focus lingered on her exposed thighs. When his gaze returned to her face, he spotted a hint of defiance in her eyes, as if she expected him to disapprove of something.

"Ready for our afternoon session?" he asked.

Without a word, she turned and walked away. Something was annoying her. He'd discover what it was shortly. Instead of following her, he made his way into the small kitchen and opened the refrigerator.

They'd found a small kitchen in the cabins helped the couples feel more at home. He glanced at the table, where a platter with fruit, cheese, and sandwiches sat there along with water and juice.

Good. His instructions had been carried out as directed. Closing the refrigerator, he sauntered to the doorway of the bedroom where Becca had disappeared.

Becca stood by the window, hugging herself. He glanced at the disheveled bed.

Ah, that's why she's upset. And that's why she looked so flustered when she opened the door.

"Someone has been masturbating."

"It helps a little bit," she muttered. Then in a stronger voice. "I want a vibrator."

Tyler crossed over to her, slipped his arms around her, and tugged her back against him. "After the toy class tomorrow."

"Today."

A demand?

"No." He was firm. "We've had issues in the past where clients used some of our toys without proper instruction and ended up in the ER. We keep them locked until after the class."

"Damn it, Tyler." She twisted in his hold until she faced him. "I need a vibrator."

"I can be your vibrator." Guiding her, he walked backward to the bed. "Tell me your fantasies."

"Right now, it's roasting you over a fire pit."

He laughed. "At least you're honest." There was the spunky woman he remembered from college. "But not so fun for me."

"This isn't funny." She squirmed in his hold.

"I can remedy that." He released her and toed off his shoes, then pulled his shirt over his head.

"What are you doing?" She stood, defiant, with her fists jammed on her hips.

"Undressing. Are you going to join me, or do you want me to peel those clothes off you—one item at a time?"

"Do it."

There was a note of challenge in her voice. She was daring him, and he had no intention of backing down. He finished undressing, deliberately taking his time, folded his clothes precisely —again in no rush—and placed them on top of the dresser. His cock was now fully erect. He could feel her gaze boring into his skin. He turned and a soft gasp left her lips.

"Ummmm...it's...ahh...bigger than I remember."

"Could be." In a few steps, he was in front of her. Leaning down, his lips hovered above hers. "I've been jacking off since yesterday, and it hasn't helped me either."

His mouth closed over hers in a soft kiss. He was going to savor every minute. He'd make her come, but on *his* terms. Catching the hem of her T-shirt, he lifted.

He held their kiss until the last second, before he whisked the fabric over her head. He tossed it in the direction of the dresser. "No bra." He palmed her bare breast, massaging it before moving to the other one. Her nipples were already hard.

"It was irritating my nipples."

"Your skin is silky smooth." He trailed his fingers down her sides to the waistband of her shorts. He hooked his thumbs inside the fabric. "Nice short-shorts."

She shifted from one foot to the other. "Take them off."

He unhooked the button and edged the zipper down, then peeled the fabric over her hips. Her musky scent tantalized his nose as he stripped her panties with her shorts. He tossed them out of the way, not caring where they landed.

"You are so beautiful."

She squirmed beneath his gaze, then shivered when his palms covered her hips, his thumbs drawing lazy circles on her skin. Without hesitation, he dropped to his knees and blew out a breath, ruffling her pubic curls.

"Tyler."

A tremor rippled through her body. Since he didn't want her legs giving out on her, he rose to his feet, scooped her up, and placed her on the bed. Before he could move, she ran her fingers up and down his hard cock.

"Hard, but warm," she murmured. "And definitely much bigger than I remember."

"It's all yours," he whispered as he laid down next to her. Pushing the stray hair away from her ear, he licked the lobe. "What's your fantasy for today?"

***

Becca bit her lower lip. She couldn't believe how forthright she'd been with Tyler, but then again, she'd never been so frustrated in all her life. Even now, he nuzzled the skin below her ear, causing delicious shivers of pleasure to run through her body.

"I want..." She cleared her throat. "I want you to lick and suck me all over."

"That sounds like fun." His lips caressed her neck, his tongue leaving a light wet trail, until he found the spot where her neck and shoulder met. He sucked, then blew air on her skin.

Becca moaned. *Oh, my goodness.*

"Good moan or bad moan?" The words were muffled against her skin.

"Good one." Oh, so good.

His mouth continued its journey, dropping kisses on her collar bone, on her right shoulder, and down her arm. He kissed each finger in turn.

Becca fought against squirming, her senses totally focused on Tyler's lips. Each touch, lick, or nip caused more moisture to gather between her thighs.

"I'll use my hands too." His voice sounded thick with desire.

Tremors swept through her as he lightly raked his nails over her left arm, while his tongue licked her inner right arm. His left hand found hers, and their fingers tangled together.

His tongue paused at her wrist, where her pulse pounded, before moving lower. "Ohhhh." It was more of a groan than a word as he drew her index finger between his lips and sucked.

Her pussy tightened. She was going to come from him sucking her fingers. How was that even possible? Before her body could ratchet up another notch, he released her finger.

"Now what?" That familiar sexy bad-boy grin played around his lips.

She shifted her legs, hoping to relieve the pressure.

His eyes darkened. "Tell me what you want," he demanded.

"I don't remember you being this dominant in college." Forceful at times, maybe.

"We didn't have a lot of time then. We had classes and studying, plus a party or two."

"More than a party or two," she joked. Tyler had been known to party most weekends with or without her, but he never crossed the line and cheated on her. And, somehow, he never got behind in his classes or missed a test.

"Agreed. Now we have all the time in the world."

"Just this week." She wasn't sure she could voice her needs. Too many times being shut down by men saying they didn't need her instructions had taken firm hold.

This was different. This was Tyler, and he wanted to hear her voice.

Still, something held her back. She shifted, but he didn't move. "I…" She couldn't get the words past the lump in her throat.

Lord, did the session this morning teach me nothing? While she understood communication with her partner was important, getting past her own fears proved more difficult.

"Maybe you need more warming up." His mouth closed over her right nipple.

Oh fuck. He nipped at her flesh, making her pussy tighten. When he switched to her other breast, she could barely catch her breath. Then he stopped and pushed her thighs apart, cradling her knees in his arms.

Yes, that's what I want. His breath brushed against her overheated skin. She glanced at him from beneath her lashes to find him studying her. Gazes locked, he slipped his index finger into his mouth and pulled it out with a *pop*.

He traced her labia with his wet finger before lowering his head and nipping at her inner thighs.

"Oh god," she whispered as her hips arched. She could swear she felt him smiling against her skin. Without conscious thought, her fingers tangled into the quilt covering the bed. Tyler continued to nibble, kiss, and lick her inner thighs.

Heat raced over her skin as he spread her pussy lips. Cool air played around her opening as his thumb circled her clit without touching it directly. Between the cool air and his touch, her tension ratcheted up another notch. She clutched the fabric beneath them. She needed...

"Tyler." *Did I say that aloud?*

"Yes, sweetheart?" His breath brushed over her clit, and her hips bucked. She wanted him, his lips on her clit, his tongue caressing her until she came.

"Please." Damn, she was begging.

"Please what?"

She wanted to smack him, but instead she said, "Please lick my pussy."

"My pleasure." His tongue swept over her clit from top to bottom.

"Yes!" she shouted. She expected him to dive right in, but instead, he circled her clit, then his finger followed the path of his tongue.

"You taste so sweet. Sweeter than when we were in college." He slipped his finger into her pussy, prompting her to moan. "Wetter too." A second finger joined the first. "You're sopping, and I love it."

"Yes, please." Her hips arched, pressing toward his fingers, wanting more.

"I like you wet. I like it when you're flushed with desire and need. Most of all, I want you on edge, begging for it."

His mouth covered her clit, his tongue flicking it as he wiggled his fingers within her. She cried out as her muscles clamped down on those wonderful digits that made her nerves tingle. She wanted to come so bad.

Her orgasm was right there, hanging, waiting for the right touch, the right movement that would send her over the edge. But Tyler wasn't doing that. He stilled his fingers inside her until her pussy stopped gripping them.

He moved them once again, and as soon as she tightened around them, he'd stop. Again and again.

"More." She could barely get the word out. "I need more." The need in her voice scared her, but only for a mere second. It wasn't fear of Tyler. It was fear of being left unsatisfied, as she'd had been with other men.

Tyler added a third finger as he drew her clit into his mouth. A shudder rippled through her body. A good one.

She really hadn't anticipated these eye-opening sensations. When he curved his fingers and tapped her G-spot, her tummy tightened and her toes curled.

"Fuck!" she yelled as her climax rolled over her in unforgiving waves, her fingers clutching the quilt beneath her. It wasn't until the first hard waves subsided that she realized Tyler continued to lick her clit with slow strokes, and his fingers remained inside her clenching pussy.

He wiggled them. "Tyler, I don't think—" The words came out slowly while she fought to catch her breath. But he started stroking her pussy once again.

She couldn't...but she could. Her pussy quivered. Becca released the quilt and buried her fingers in his hair when his tongue flicked her clit. Her second climax hit, and her hips arched, pressing against his mouth and fingers.

"I..." She'd never had multiple orgasms until now, and it felt like she couldn't breathe. Her head thrashed against the mattress while Tyler slowly eased up, and the tremors faded. Becca released his head and collapsed against the mattress. She was totally spent.

And damn if she hadn't enjoyed everything he'd done to her.

***

Tyler lifted his head and licked his lips, tasting Becca's unique flavor. Her body had gone limp beneath him, and he couldn't help the pride swelling in him that he'd made her orgasm twice.

She was fantastic. So responsive to his touch, and she tasted so sweet. Glancing up at her, he took in her parted lips, the rise and fall of her chest, her nipples at full attention. He was tempted to take those taut peaks into his mouth and suck for all he was worth.

His fingers remained in her pussy as she spasmed around them. Eventually, with care, he slid his fingers from her and began kissing his way up her body, making sure to keep his full weight off of her.

Becca opened her eyes, and he recognized not only satisfaction in her gaze, but desire. Without hesitation, he leaned down and covered her lips with his. His cock jumped when he realized she probably tasted herself on his lips

Her lips parted, and he thrust his tongue into the recesses of her mouth, teasing and tasting her. He wanted to dive into her hot, wet core, but he wouldn't. Today was about communication, building trust, and her satisfaction. His could wait.

He broke the kiss, and her sigh brushed against his skin. Her fingers dug into his shoulders.

"You're so beautiful," he whispered, rolling onto his side and cradling her against him.

"I've never..." She closed her eyes, concealing her gaze from him.

Tyler waited. She would talk when she was ready. Their gazes connected once again as she stared at him.

"You've improved with age. I've never had multiple orgasms before."

"You'll have a lot more of them before we're through." He was pleased she trusted him enough to tell him about her orgasms. In college, he'd been more interested in his satisfaction than his hers.

He'd learned a lot about how to satisfy a woman. His stomach rumbled, Becca giggled.

"I think someone's hungry."

While he didn't want to leave her luscious body, it was time to feed another hunger. "Be right back." He dropped a kiss on her rosy lips and slid off the bed.

Once in the kitchen, picked up the large platter of food, then grabbed two bottles of water and returned to the bedroom. A naked picnic in bed sounded good to him.

But Becca wasn't in bed where he left her.

She was wearing her robe and standing by the window. He fought to hide his disappointment.

Give her time. They might have known each other in the past, but this was a different time and place. They'd matured and changed.

"Shall we go and eat on the back porch?"

"Sure." Becca shrugged, but didn't look at him.

That's not good. His gut clenched. Balancing the food, he pushed open the French doors and stepped outside. He set the platter on the side table along with the water, then crossed to where Becca stood in the doorway.

Without a word, he framed her face with his hands and gave her a hard, deep kiss. Once he finished, they were both breathing hard. He gazed at her upturned face, seeing her desire, but there was something else—a hint of fear, maybe. He reined in his needs. Communication was important.

"Sit down." He gestured to the porch swing.

"Ummm... Aren't you going to put something on?"

"No." He was fine with being nude. He sat on the swing and waited for her to join him.

"But..." Her gaze shifted to his rock-hard cock, and it jumped. "What about the people next door?"

"We have complete privacy." He gestured to the hedges. It was one of the things he and Jared made sure of when they laid out the cabins and landscaping.

She studied the hedges. "I see it now." Instead of taking a seat on the swing, Becca chose to sit in the chair across from him.

Masking his disappointment, he grabbed a sandwich and bit into it. "Eat something." He hadn't eaten since breakfast, and he needed to keep his strength up. He had a feeling Becca was going to test him at every turn.

Her silence weighed on him as he ate. He waited to see what she would do, but she only sat with her hands folded neatly into her lap. This was the closed-down Becca he disliked.

"Why did you put the robe on?" He wanted her to at least talk to him. He twisted the caps off the water bottles before taking one and drinking.

"I can't run around naked."

"Sure you can."

Her head tilted, and a giggle escaped her lips before she sobered once again. "I sound like my mother."

"Tell me about her." Tyler sat back. During their time in college, her mother called her constantly, but Becca never really talked much about her, nor had he met her mother.

"My mother is a piece of work." She sighed. "You remember in college how often she called me?"

He nodded. "I remember being surprised you were living in an apartment near campus on your own."

"Yeah, I wanted to pretend my mother didn't exist because college meant freedom."

"I'm sorry." He'd been too self-absorbed with school and everything to think about why she didn't talk about her mother.

"After you left, the calls got more frequent. When I graduated, she insisted I move back home."

"And did you?" He wanted her to keep talking.

She crossed her arms over her stomach, and her features tightened. Did she even realize how much she was telling him with her body?

Probably not.

"For a while. I knew it was a mistake, but I needed to build my resume first." She tightened her arms around her waist.

Tyler almost stood to pull her into his lap and cradle her close. Her closed expression and the way she held herself told him whatever had happened wasn't good.

"My mother has always been controlling."

"What about your father?" She'd never mentioned him.

We should have talked more in college.

"I don't know. All my mother would ever say was that he wasn't around."

It hit Tyler right then. She said *my mother*, not *my mom.* "I'm sorry."

She gave him a little smile. "After I moved back home, Mother became even more obsessed with controlling every aspect of my life."

"That couldn't have been easy. You'd been on your own for four years in college."

"It wasn't. As my mother said, I'd grown an attitude."

"I bet." He couldn't see Becca kowtowing to anyone.

"At least, that's what she would tell me. Anyway, without my knowledge, she arranged a job for me." Becca snorted; there was no other way for him to describe it. "I should have realized there was no way a person like me, straight out of college with only a bachelor's degree and no experience, should have landed that job as head of catering at the Franco Hotel."

Tyler whistled. That was one of the premier hotels in San Francisco. "You were excited."

"Yes, and afraid. But my excitement overrode the fear, and things were fine until..."

He waited. He was starting to get the picture, and he was sure he wouldn't like where this was going. "Until?" he prompted.

"Until Randall."

"Randall, not Alan?"

"Yeah, he was before Alan." Another sigh escaped her. "I was so stupid, Tyler. So damn naïve. After you left, I wasn't really interested in being with another man."

"This Randall entered your life." He fought his own jealousy. He'd had other lovers during their time apart. Why shouldn't she?

"Yes. He was older, and I couldn't believe he was interested in me."

"How much older?"

"Ten years."

Not a huge gap. "I can see why any man with a brain would be interested in you."

"Thanks." She bit her lower lip. "I started dating Randall. At first, it was fun, then Mother started pressuring me to marry him."

"Did you?" She hadn't mentioned being married before, only leaving her ex—Alan.

"No, but it was damn close. I can see now what happened with perfect clarity, but back then, I guess I didn't want to see it at the time." Her voice quivered.

Tyler clenched his hands. He had to let her tell the story in her own way.

"Did you know that going to SF State was the first time I defied my mother's will?" Her voice was soft.

"No." He wished they'd had this conversation about her mother years ago. "Because I was clueless and I regret not asking."

"I didn't want to discuss my mother and you didn't push. I was happy living in my bubble. "Everything I did in high school was because of my mother. After I graduated, Mother wanted me to be a part of her ladies groups, charities, and all that."

"You had other ideas."

"Yes. I wanted to study hotel hospitality. SF State was the perfect place. I had the grades, and I even had several scholarships lined up. When I told my mother, she went ballistic." Becca shivered.

Tyler could see it. An eighteen-year-old Becca standing up to her domineering mother for the first time.

"She yelled and raged at me, and for once, I let it all bounce off me. Everything I'd done up until that time was to please my mother. I held my ground, and when fall arrived, I moved into a small apartment right by campus."

He'd noticed her the second day of classes. How he missed her in high school Tyler didn't know. She sat two rows over from him in a marketing class, but it wasn't until months later that he finally asked her out.

"My mother never knew I had a lover in college." Becca seemed to curl into herself. She drew her legs up and wrapped her arms around them. "Randall and I had been dating about six months when he asked me to marry him. I was going to say no, but he told me he'd already spoken to Mother. Not wanting to disappoint her, I agreed. My first mistake."

Her breathing quickened. "The second one was two months later. One night he took me back to his place—not unusual, we would often go to his place, sit, and talk."

"This night was different?" His heart hurt as his anger at her mother and this Randall person grew.

"Yes. I'd been dragging my feet about the wedding date. Mother was pressuring me, and so was Randall. All I wanted to do was run away. That alone should have clued me in that something wasn't right." She stood and paced a few steps before turning back to him.

When he spotted the agony in her features, he stood and moved to her side and pulled her into his arms. He would give her as much comfort as he could.

"I was so stupid." Her voice trembled.

He couldn't stand hearing her put herself down for something that wasn't her fault. "Not stupid," he countered.

"Why didn't I see what was coming?" She hiccupped. "I trusted him."

"*Shhhh*." He cradled her closer. He hated she was so upset. "You don't have to tell me."

"I do." She leaned back in his embrace and gazed up at him.

The tears in her eyes tugged at his heart.

"Communication is important. You need to know this before we go any further, and I need to tell you."

Tyler nodded but wouldn't release her. He'd share his strength for whatever she had to say.

"It started off innocent enough, kissing and light petting, but then Randall got aggressive."

"He assaulted you?" That was the only conclusion he could come to.

"Almost." Her voice was barely a whisper now. "I fought him. Hard. I wasn't ready. He ripped my clothing and hit me. While I was dazed, he threw me onto the bed. He was holding me down when my cell rang."

Fucking bastard. Tyler tightened his arms around her. He'd make sure he had the rat bastard's full name and then send some friends to see Randall and remind him how to treat a woman.

"It was probably the only time I was grateful for my mother calling me. It gave me a chance to push Randall off. I grabbed my phone and screamed at my mother to call the police."

"And did she?"

Becca's eyes filled with anger and disappointment. "She demanded I give the phone to Randall. I did, thinking she'd tell him to back off. He placed the phone on the table and tapped speaker." Her body shook. "My mother told Randall he couldn't fuck me, but he could check to see if I was still a virgin any way he wanted."

"Son of a bitch." Damn. Her mother was a piece of work. It was a good thing he didn't hurt women, but he damn sure wanted to hurt that woman. As for Randall, Tyler's decision to have his friends give him a talking-to was cemented.

"I was so shocked by my mother's words that I wasn't prepared when Randall forced me back on the bed." She paused and took a deep breath. "Something inside me broke in that moment. I screamed at the top of my lungs and startled Randall. So I pushed him off, pulled my ripped shirt together, and ran out of his apartment.

"Shit." He could picture her outside, trembling and afraid, half-dressed.

"That's how I met Angie. I ran to a nearby coffee shop. She was coming out and asked me what was wrong. I could barely get the words out. Angie realized at once what had happened. She loaded me into her car and took me to her apartment. She was my angel that night."

Tyler made a mental note to thank Angie somehow. She saved Becca.

"The next day, Angie and her boyfriend went with me to my mother's house. I think it helped she was dating a guy who worked in construction, and she brought her two huge older brothers with us. They helped me pack my belongings. The whole time, my mother raged at me that the night before was all a misunderstanding. I told her it wasn't and walked out."

"You moved in with Angie?"

"Yes. For the longest time, I couldn't stand to be alone."

"I'm so sorry this all happened." He gathered her close, wanting so much to do something more. But what could he do?

"I'm not done yet. I showed up for work the next day, and that's when I found out my mother had secured the job for me. All of a sudden, I was enemy number one at work, and then I was called into my supervisor's office. Randall stood there and accused me of sleeping with him to get a better position and that the only reason I had the position was because of my mother."

"That is unfair."

"Yes. But I was so tired of everything, I quit my job and walked away. If it hadn't been for Angie, I don't know what I would have done."

"When I meet Angie, I'm going to give her a big hug for taking care of you and for sending you to me." Becca's head rested on his shoulder. He held her close, wanting to take all her pain away.

"She's my best friend for a reason. Needless to say, I found a new job and began working my way up. And last week, my dream job as head of catering at the Palace Hotel became available. It's always been out of my reach. But now it's mine."

Becca had always talked about how the Palace Hotel was one of the best places to be for job growth. *I can't stand in the way of her happiness.* This was a one week deal, and he needed to remember that. "What about the ex?" He really didn't want to ask, but he needed to know.

"Alan? I already told you about him." She relaxed against him, letting him take her weight as if she was exhausted from all the talking.

"Tell me how you acquired your battery-operated boyfriend." He wanted to lighten the mood and get her mind off her mother and her past.

Becca laughed, and Tyler's heart lightened. "Angie, of course. She introduced me to an adult store. She helped me understand it was okay to have sexual needs, and how to satisfy myself."

"Yet you've been suppressing your sexuality for years."

"Yes." She raised her head and looked at him. "While having a vibrator helped, I still kept my needs under tight control. It wasn't until I saw Alan in bed with my boss that I realized how much I'd been suppressing. Then I came here and saw you… the feelings you re-ignited in me made it clear how utterly wrong Alan was for me. I've never felt this way about another man. Only you, Tyler." She took a breath.

Tyler was stunned and couldn't think of anything to say.

"I watched you with the horse. They way you stroked her body, the way you spoke softly to her, and your patience. Even all these years later, you're different, but then so am I. You generously agreed to be my partner and helped me free the woman inside me. There was the man I could trust."

Her unfettered trust in him made his heart pound. It also worried him. It was a lot to live up to, and he knew he couldn't get too close to her. Any attachment would fail. She had her dream job awaiting her, and he wouldn't compete with that. He'd done it before and lost. "I can promise you I will never hurt you, never force you. There are reasons for a safe word."

"And what is my safe word?"

"Pick one. Something you won't say in the heat of passion, yet something that will get my attention."

Her nose scrunched up as she thought, then she grinned. "Tomato."

"Perfect."

"Now what?"

"Let's get rid of this robe." Tyler undid the belt and slid the fabric from her shoulders. "Now tell me what you want."

***

Becca fought to control her breathing as Tyler trailed his hands up and down her spine after removing her robe. When she told him what had happened with Randall, a weight lifted from her. For once, her trust in someone was on point. He supported her. Angie had been the only other person to do that. Her heart stuttered with the knowledge.

"I want..." She licked her lips in anticipation. It was time to shed her old self and let her new self shine. Tyler wouldn't judge her wants or needs. "I want to suck your cock. To make you come for me." She pushed against his shoulders, and he took several steps back until the chair forced him to sit.

She grabbed a pillow from the other patio chair, dropped it at his feet to pad her knees, knelt, and parted his legs. She grasped the base of his cock in one hand. "Hard as steel, yet soft." With the other hand, she lightly traced up one side and down the other, her index finger barely touching his skin. With each movement, she exhaled and her breath teased his cock. His cock twitched. Hiding a grin, she stuck her tongue out and licked him from tip to base and back.

Tyler groaned, and his hands tightened over the arms of the chair. Power surged through her.

"I can feel you pulsing against my tongue." She dotted kisses along his dick before finding his balls and kissing them too.

"Damn it, Becca." His fingers tangled in her hair. Not pushing her away or pulling her toward him. This man had so much control. She hoped she could make him lose it.

Shifting, she lowered her mouth to his cock and used her tongue to play with his overheated skin, savoring his salty taste.

"Oh yes, sweetheart." His hips shifted. "Suck me."

She traced her nails traced over his balls as she drew him deeper into her mouth. He was bigger than she remembered from college. And she wanted to take him all. Relaxing her throat, her tongue danced around him as she hollowed her cheeks.

"That's it, baby," he whispered.

His words gave her the encouragement to keep going. She hadn't sucked a man since Tyler. She hadn't wanted to until now. His fingers guided her, his hips tense but she kept her same pace and Tyler groaned.

"God, baby, that feels so good."

She gently nipped at his tip, then took him deep once again. His balls tightened beneath her fingers as she caressed them.

"Baby, I can't last much longer."

Satisfaction flowed through her over his words. Becca didn't want him to last. She wanted to taste his pleasure, to make him come.

Raising her head, she let his cock slip free from her lips. "Let go." Then she took him all the way in, her fingers rolling his balls. When he thrust his hips, she followed and kept sucking him. She'd take everything he had to give her.

He cried out and started pulsing into her mouth. His familiar taste rolled over her tongue, slightly salty and pure male. He held her head still, but she didn't fight him. Instead, she kept sucking and stroking his balls until he was spent, and his cock softened.

Becca released him from her mouth with a *pop* and smiled in satisfaction.

"Witch." He grasped her by the elbows and lifted her into his lap, covering her mouth with his even as his musky taste still filled her senses. Their tongues danced, and Becca squirmed on his lap, trying to find a way to straddle him. She wanted his dick inside her.

A loud bell rang.

She reared back, almost falling off Tyler's lap. "What the hell was that?"

"Warning bell." A soft curse left his lips. "Jared's idea of giving the guests a reminder that dinner is in an hour."

"Why haven't I heard it before today?"

"He only uses it once classes start."

"We still have time." She wiggled in his lap.

"Not yet, sweetheart." He captured her lips with one more kiss and then stood with her in his arms. "Shower, then dinner."

Chapter Eight

♥

Becca woke alone the next morning. *How the hell did Tyler get away from me last night?* He'd carried her into the cabin, deposited her in her shower, and told her he'd see her at dinner. Then after dinner, he kissed her at her cabin door and told her he'd see her this morning in the lecture.

Frustrated, she'd slept fitfully, wanting Tyler there beside her. Hell, inside her pussy, fucking her brains out. She hadn't felt this needy in a long time.

Then there was the note she found under her door this morning. *Please dress comfortably in loose clothing for the toy lecture. Underwear is optional.*

Optional? Was this someone's idea of a joke? Her nipples were hard, but she wasn't crazy enough to advertise it. Nope. Underwear was a must. Becca surveyed the clothing she'd brought with her, settling for a pair of yoga pants and a T-shirt.

A quick look at the clock told her she had just enough time to grab coffee and food before the lecture. She had a feeling she would need both. When she walked into the lecture room, she hoped to find Tyler.

No such luck. Charlie and Sally were there, along with Peter and Maggie. Becca sat on the mat with the other couples, wondering where the hell Tyler was. She chatted with the other couples for a few minutes, and then her body went on full alert.

"Good morning, all." She turned her head to see Tyler walking into the room with a large box in his arms.

What the hell?

"Today, we're going to talk about toys for both men and women. Give me a few minutes to set things up, and we'll get started." After he set the box on the table, he opened it and began removing items.

She bit her lower lip. *Tyler's the instructor? I didn't see this one coming.* This would be an interesting lecture.

He glanced up, and his gaze captured hers. Damn, if this man's sexual desire didn't show in his eyes.

"For your information, the cabinets in the cabins have now been unlocked." Tyler winked at her, and her body flushed. "So, let's start with your standard vibrator."

***

Tyler didn't bother to knock on Becca's cabin door, knowing it was unlocked, because after the lecture, he told her to leave it that way. He walked in and was surprised that she wasn't sitting in the main area, waiting for him.

She couldn't hide her surprise when he walked into the classroom, especially when she realized he was the one giving the lecture. But that wasn't the last of her surprises for the morning. The other two couples weren't as shy as Becca. They'd played and tried out several of the toys while in class.

Poor Becca. She was really getting an education. He strode into her bedroom and found her sitting on the edge of the bed, staring at the now unlocked and open cabinet.

"There's a heck of a lot more in here than what we talked about today." Her gaze never left the cabinet.

"Yes." He stood beside the bed. "Remember, I said there would be items for bondage and submission, along with anal penetration."

Her hand moved to her throat. "Will..." She cleared her throat. "Will we use all of them?"

"If you want. Your choice, your pleasure." He slipped his arm around her shoulders as he sat next to her. "We still have more lectures to attend and time to play. What would you like to try first?"

When she didn't speak, he wondered if he was pushing too hard.

"I'll grab some water and food out of the fridge," he offered to give her a moment. "Why don't you take out what you want to play with, and I'll be right back."

He dropped a light kiss on her lips before leaving the room. Tyler wanted her to be comfortable with what they were doing. This had to be her decision.

***

Becca watched Tyler walk away, grateful for a few minutes to find her composure. Her hands shook as she removed some toys from the cabinet. There were several she wanted to know more about before she tried them.

She remembered others from class, such as the butt plugs. After setting them on the nightstand, she strode over to the French doors taking a moment to collect herself and enjoy the view. During class, the other couples were uninhibited and tried several of the toys, even with an audience. It had excited her, and she wasn't sure if that was a good thing or not.

She turned from the door as Tyler walked into the room with two bottles of water and a fruit platter. He glanced at the nightstand, his grin widening as he took in what she'd laid out.

"I'd like you to explain some of these to me." She was proud that her voice hadn't quavered.

"Sure." He set the water and fruit on the dresser, then picked up the odd-shaped dildo that had a squeeze ball on one end, a set of small beads on a string, and an odd-looking skinny thing. "These three we'll talk about after the anal lecture." He returned them to the cabinet.

Well, that answers one question. She sighed. No wonder she didn't have a clue what they were. Her heart stuttered. Anal. While it sounded exciting, she wasn't sure she was ready to do it.

Yet.

Tyler took out three different vibrators, a bullet-shaped object, some sort of jewelry, and several other items and set them on the nightstand.

A shiver slid up her spine.

Is that excitement or apprehension? Excitement, she decided, as her gut clenched and moisture gathered between her thighs.

"Pick the first item you want me to explain, but"—the *but* made her hesitate—"be prepared. If I decide it's something for us to use, we will use it."

"You decide?" This was a switch from yesterday.

"Yes. I'm your partner. While we will decide most things together, I want to give you pleasure. You need to explore the toys and how they feel, so I'll make the decision. You have your safe word."

Biting her lip, Becca stood there, staring at the toys. What was the sense of having Tyler as her partner if she wasn't willing to trust him? She picked up what looked like a weird vibrator. It was curved near the top where a small round shaped ball sat. At the end of the ball, there were tiny nubs.

"That's a vibrating prostate stimulator." His hand covered hers. "This is for a man."

"I wondered how a woman would get pleasure from this." Part of her was surprised he'd left it on the table for her to examine.

"You can use this to stimulate my prostate either manually or with the vibrator, or"—he lightly stroked the nubs with his fingertips—"the nubs can be used to press against the perineum, making me come harder than you've seen."

"You'd let me use this on you?" She hadn't expected that.

"If you wanted to, but not today." He took the toy from her and returned it to the cabinet. "Next?"

Looking over the items, Becca picked up another one. "I know these are handcuffs, but why are there suction cups attached to them."

"These are made so I can cuff you to any smooth surface." He slipped his arm around her waist and pulled her close. "I can use them in the shower, on the window, a wall, on the hood of my small pickup truck."

"The hood of your truck?" Why did that idea make her shiver with anticipation?

"Oh, yeah." He maneuvered her until his hard cock pressed against her. "Think about it. You're naked, hands cuffed over your head, your nipples pointing toward the sky. Your legs dangle over the edge, and you can't touch the ground. I slip between your thighs, holding you open. You're completely helpless to anything I want to do, but I start off slowly, putting your legs on my shoulders and licking your creaming pussy."

Her muscles clenched at the picture he painted.

"Once you've come on my tongue, I'll straighten and bury my hard dick in you on the first thrust. You'll cry out from the shock and pleasure. I'll caress your tits as I fuck you, long and hard and take you to heights you've never known."

Her knees gave way. If he hadn't been holding her, she would have crumpled at his feet. She couldn't catch her breath.

"You're excited."

"Yes." She couldn't...wouldn't deny it. He did that to her.

"Good." He plucked the cuffs from her fingers. "Next?"

Becca forced her knees to hold her weight and reached for the next toy she wanted. If she wasn't careful, she would climax without him even touching her. She held out the piece of material to him by the two handles.

"Ah, the doggie harness."

"A what?" She dropped it into his outstretched hand. "If you use that on a dog, why is it here?"

Tyler's laughter filled the room, and she glared at him. "It's not for a dog, sweetheart." He maneuvered her in front of him. "Bend over and place your palms on the mattress."

Without thinking, she did as he directed. The next thing she knew, the harness was around her waist. "Tyler?"

"Remember when I used to take you from behind? Doggie position."

"Yes, but..." He pulled her back by the harness, her ass meeting his erection through his sweatpants. Her breath rushed out of her at the contact. Excitement built in her veins.

"This will allow me to ride you hard and long in doggie position, giving me full control and greater range of motion than we ever had."

"Clever." She ground her ass against him.

"Behave." Laughter tinged his voice as he released her from the harness.

When she turned, he pointed to a black piece sitting in the corner that she assumed was an oversized cushion. "This is made so I can put you in any position on the bed or on the floor. It comes with wrist and ankle restraints."

Becca studied the cushion while he put the harness and handcuffs back in the cabinet. Yes, she could see it now. It could be a small piece of furniture. Very clever.

"Now for the rest of these, I'll explain them once we're both naked."

Tyler didn't wait for her; he began stripping. Becca stood watching as his delicious chest came into view.

"Slowpoke." He lifted her T-shirt up and over her head. "Pretty lacy bra, but it's time for it to go." He removed her bra and tossed it across the room, along with her T-shirt. "That's much better." His palms cupped her breasts, and she sucked in a breath at the heat from his touch. "Your skin is so soft and sensitive."

She arched her back, pushing her breasts into his hands as her eyes fluttered shut.

"Look at me."

She ignored his words and touched his chest, her fingers exploring the hard planes as her nails scraped over his flat brown nipples.

"Open. Your. Eyes." That was a command.

Her gaze connected with his. "I need to see your eyes and hear your voice. Communication between partners."

"Your touch feels so good." She swallowed. "You feel so good."

His hands traveled over her abdomen to the waistband of her pants. He pushed the fabric down along with her panties until it pooled at her feet.

"You still have your pants on." She was so caught up, she hadn't noticed until her fingers encountered fabric.

"Take them off."

She found the tie of his sweats and loosened it. Breathing hard, she pushed them down over his hips. His cock sprang free between them, hard and wanting.

"Commando," she whispered, her fingers trailing over his dick.

Tyler groaned, and Becca pulled her hand back.

"That was a good groan, sweetheart." He kissed her nose and kicked his clothing away.

Chapter Nine

♥

"What shall we try first?" Tyler fought hard to keep his libido under control. He wanted nothing better than to throw her on the bed and fuck her until they were both exhausted.

Later, he promised himself. Right now, there was a lot more he had to teach her.

She slipped around him and picked up a silver chain with several beads hanging from it.

He grinned. Becca wasn't shying away from anything.

"I'm not sure how this works." She slipped her fingers through the chain loop and let it dangle.

"It's a cock lariat." He forced the words past his dry throat. His dick was so damned hard and getting harder by the second. This toy would torment him, but this was for Becca. He spread his feet, straightened his spine, and pushed his hips forward. "Take the chain loop and slip it over the head of my cock."

Her touch felt soft and cool against his overheated skin. He kept his gaze on her fingers as she worked the chain over his glistening head. "Now gently tighten the loop until it's snug below the head and then let the rest of the chain hang loose."

She released the chain, and his head dropped back. The beads weren't heavy but tugged just enough to make him grit his teeth. Each step he took would be torment and tease his need, and he looked forward to it because it would make Becca happy.

"If I wasn't already hard, I would be now." He dragged air into his lungs. "Now it's my turn." He picked up what he wanted and held them up for her to see. "Do you remember what these are?"

"Nipple danglers." Her eyes widened, bright with excitement.

"Glad you remembered. They won't pinch or hurt." He touched her shoulder. "But first, we need to get you ready."

"Ready?" Her breathing increased, and her pupils dilated. All signs of arousal.

"Yes. Sit on the bed, sweetheart." He guided her to a straight back chair, and once she sat, he spread her thighs. Tyler dropped to his knees between her legs. Her pussy glistened with wetness, and he bit back a smile. Her hands closed over his shoulders.

"I need very erect nipples." He lowered his head. Her back arched as his tongue toyed with her right nipple, working it into a tight nub. "Since these are non-piercing rings, I'm going to place the first one over your nipple and squeeze." His actions followed his words.

Becca moaned as he took her other nipple into his mouth, and once the nipple was hard, did the same thing. He captured her gaze with his and then he let the danglers drop.

"Oh, my goodness." Her back arched.

Tyler rose to his feet and pulled her up. The movement caused them both to moan.

"How?" She took a deep breath. "How can they do that?"

"Do what?" He wanted to hear what she was feeling.

"The weight of the beads are teasing my nipples, making them harder, but it's like a direct line to my clit."

"I'm not surprised." He glanced at the other dangler on the table. Was she ready for it? He slipped his hand over her mound and penetrated her with one finger. She was drenched.

"Oh, yes. Touch me." She pressed her body against him.

"I want to try something. Do you trust me?" He wiggled his finger.

"I do."

Tyler removed his finger and picked up the clit clamp. It wouldn't hurt, only arouse her even more.

"Where are you putting that?" Anticipation made it hard to form the words.

"I'm going to slip it over your clit and let the beads hang down." This one had an elongated attachment to fit over her clit. His cock jumped and he barely held back a groan as the beads shifted.

Becca shifted from one foot to the other. Her stomach contracted, and there was a fine sheen of perspiration on her skin.

"Spread your legs, please." She widened her stance. He knelt and, using one hand, spread her pussy lips, revealing her hard clit. He slipped the clamp on and then released the beads.

"*Ahhh.*" She threw her head back, drawing in air through her nose. "Oh god. It feels... I don't know how to describe it."

He wasn't surprised by her reaction. Now to turn it up a notch.

"Let's dance." He drew her into his arms and began waltzing around the bedroom.

Her eyes grew wide as they danced, the danglers teasing her nipples and clit. His cock was hard as a rock as the lariat teased him. The beads would create just enough pressure to keep them both on edge and wanting more.

When he executed a deep dip and brought her back level, an unexpected gasp was torn from her lips. Tyler pulled her against him as her body started to tremble with an orgasm. Pride filled him that he could make her come so easily. Her orgasm subsided, and he started dancing once again.

"Oh goodness."

"Feel good?" He gazed down at her upturned face as they danced, never missing a step.

"So good. I'm already climbing toward another orgasm." She glanced down. "But what about you?"

His cock bounced, making him grit his teeth. "This is for you." He did a complicated set of turns.

"I'm going to come again." Her heavy breathing was music to his ears.

"That's the idea." He swung her in his arms.

"But..." She threw her head back as her climax ripped through her. When the tremors stopped, he picked her up and carried her to the bed.

***

The sheets felt good against Becca's overheated skin. She wanted to soak in the coolness, but Tyler parted her legs. His fingers spread her lips and then he removed the clit clamp.

Her body shuddered as his fingers danced their way up her body to her breasts. Every nerve felt alive, reacting to his lightest touch. With sure movements, he removed the nipple danglers.

Everything in her tingled with need. Their gazes collided. The needy desire in his gaze gave her the courage she needed. She needed this. Becca sat up and turned around until his cock aligned with her mouth. Carefully, she removed the cock lariat and drew him between her lips.

"Oh yes."

She loved the feel of his hardness in her mouth, his salty taste, his need for her. Her fingers encircled his base as she continued to suck, caressing his cock with her fingers and lips until he stiffened and spurted into her mouth.

He whispered her name while she swallowed his essence, then released him. She fell next to him on the mattress, both of them panting.

"Ready for round two?" he asked.

Becca burst out laughing. She couldn't help it. "What would round two entail?"

"You lying there with me doing all the work."

"Sounds like fun."

"My kind of fun." He reached over and picked up another toy. Nipple suckers.

She eyed the toy with excitement. She had wanted to try them in class today, but she didn't feel right baring herself in front of others, only in front of Tyler. He played with her nipples once again before he placed the suction cups over them.

Hold on. Something felt different. A chain trailed down over her abdomen, and his fingers parted her pussy lips. Then something was placed on her clit.

"What are you doing?" That was a silly question.

He grinned up at her. "I'm going to make you come."

Her mouth fell open when vibrations started. That was the last thing she expected. The cups began to suck her nipples and clit. Fire swept from her clit to her nipples, then spread out over her entire body. Her mouth opened on a silent scream.

"Talk to me," Tyler ordered.

She gnawed at her lower lip. "It feels like I have three mouths on me." When she shifted her hips right and then left, the clit sucker shifted a bit. The vibrations increased a notch. *How the hell was he doing that?*

"Wicked man," she muttered. "The ones in class didn't vibrate."

His chuckle filled her ears. "No, they didn't. But I love this wireless remote." The suction increased. Before she could say another word, her back arched as pleasure swept through her, filling every crevice of her body. And she wanted more.

She wanted *everything* Tyler could give her.

***

Tyler loved watching the look of pure bliss on Becca's face as she climaxed. He slowly turned the vibrations down until the toy was off. Her nipples and clit were going to be very sensitive after this. The second her body stopped trembling, he released the suckers and removed them.

Her hand curved around his neck, and she pulled him down for a quick, hard kiss. "Fuck me," she whispered against her lips.

There was nothing he wanted more, but this was the time to build up her pleasure. To show her what her body was capable of. He set the suckers on the nightstand and picked up a dildo. Using the head, he circled her pussy with it, allowing her wetness to coat the toy.

"How big have your previous lovers been?"

A flush rose to her cheeks. "Average, I guess. I didn't take time to measure them, but they were smaller than you." She giggled, which turned quickly into a moan as he pressed the head of the dildo into her pussy.

"You're so wet, and that's a good thing. I won't need lube."

"You make me wet." Her voice was soft.

"And you make me hot and hard." When he applied more pressure, the dildo slipped inside her. He felt her muscles tighten around the toy, and his cock jumped. With easy strokes, he pulled and pushed the toy in her pussy as his gaze settled on her flushed face. Well, her whole body was flushed.

"How does that feel?" He wanted to keep her talking.

"Hard, but not you. I still want more. Give me more."

"Let's try something different."

She moaned when he pulled the dildo from her.

"This one." She guided his hand to one of the vibrators. "All at once, I want it inside me. Show me how it would feel to have you fill me on the first thrust."

Pre-cum coated his cock, and damn if he didn't grow harder at her words. He picked up the vibrator and placed it at her entrance. Their gazes locked.

"Do it," she whispered.

His heart pounded, and he pushed in half of the vibrator. It sank into her warm depths as her hips arched toward him.

"Fuck," she screamed.

"Easy, sweetheart." He held the toy still, allowing her body to adjust around it. She was so damn tight. "Do you know how sexy you look with your pussy clenching around my toy?" He enjoyed talking to her while he brought her to orgasm. He hadn't done that with other lovers, not even with his fiancée.

Leaning over, his lips caressed her stomach as he slid the vibrator out and then in. Slowly working more of the toy into her pussy with each thrust.

"Relax your inner muscles." Her clenching the toy was making it difficult for him.

"Easy for you to say." She took a shaky breath, let it out, then took another.

"That's it." Her stomach contracted while he moved the toy.

"Oh god, Tyler, it feels so good inside my pussy, sending bolts of fire through my body. I wish it was you in me."

"Later. First, we have to prepare you. We have a lot of things to cover." It was easier to move the vibrator now.

"Like what?"

"Let's see." He glanced at the vibrator. It was almost completely inside her. *Good.* "Anal lecture, BDSM lecture, threesome-and-more lecture."

Her fingers curled into the covers as he slowly pulled the toy from her body, only to push it back in.

She panted, apparently trying to catch her breath. "And we're going to... try... all that?" Her mouth was wide open as she tried to catch her breath.

"Do you want to? It's your decision, not mine."

"Yes," she whispered as a tremor rippled through her body.

"Good, because I want to explore it all with you." He moved the vibrator faster and turned it on low.

"That feels..." Her hips arched.

"What?"

"Good. Delicious. Wicked."

"You haven't seen wicked yet." His mouth slanted over hers as he turned the vibrations up.

Her tongue dueled with his as her pussy tightened with each stroke. She cried out when Tyler angled the toy against her clit.

He smiled. The tiny nubs on the base of the vibrator rubbed her sensitive clit as her hips rose and fell with each stroke. He sensed her orgasm building. It wouldn't take much to put her over.

Breaking the kiss, he pressed the nubs against her clit as he turned the vibrator on high.

Becca screamed as she climaxed, her hands clenching and unclenching in time with her pussy. He held still and let her ride the wave. When she slumped onto the mattress, he turned the toy off, removed it from her pussy, and set it back on the nightstand.

Her eyes remained closed, but her body still shook with the aftermath.

"Becca?" He wanted to make sure she was okay.

"Give... me... a... second." The words stuttered out of her.

Tyler gathered her damp body into his arms, cradling her against his chest.

"I—" She hiccupped.

"*Shhh*. Let me take care of you." Tremors swept through her and echoed into him as he carried her to the bathroom.

"I've never climaxed so much or come that hard from a toy." She sounded breathless.

Tyler's breath caught in his throat. He'd been a selfish lover in college, but he could make it up to her now. Her pleasure would always come before his. Inside the bathroom, he set her on the edge of the tub and kept an arm around her waist when she swayed. He closed the drain and turned on the water. As the tub filled, he dropped in vanilla bath gel beads.

Once the bath was full, he gently helped her into the warm water. "Lay there and soak for a while. Relax." He straightened, and his cock bobbed with the movement.

"He needs attention." Her fingers danced over his cock.

His body tightened with desire. Not now. He wouldn't be selfish. Never again. They had a single week together, and it was all for her.

"Later, I promise." He carefully removed her fingers and left her alone to enjoy her bath.

While Becca was in the bathroom, Tyler dressed, cleaned up the toys, and put everything away. They had forty-five minutes until dinner. He plucked at his shirt. After being naked, the fabric irritated his skin. He needed some relief even if it was from his own hand.

"Becca, dinner is in forty-five minutes," he called out. "I'm going to go clean up. I'll meet you at the lodge."

"Okay."

"Soak for at least another twenty minutes. You're going to feel those muscles we used today." He chuckled when she spouted outrage.

Life is so much better with Becca in it.

Chapter Ten

♥

Becca winced as she dressed. Tyler was right. She was sore in places she never expected. Of course, it didn't help that her clit tingled with each step she took, and she had to leave her bra off because her nipples were so sensitive. Thank goodness, she had a heavier shirt that would conceal her braless state.

She walked slowly into the dining room and wondered how Tyler was faring, considering his hard state when he left her. Tyler stood by the table, and when he saw her, he made a beeline to her.

Without a word, he cupped her chin and captured her lips, plundering her mouth. There was no other way to describe it. When he broke the kiss his eyes glittered and they were both breathing hard.

The sound of masculine chuckles and female sighs brought Becca back to the present with a jolt. Jared stood at the head of the table with a big grin on his face, and all the other couples were already seated.

Heat crept up her body to her face. She almost buried her burning cheeks against Tyler's chest, but they were all adults. Consenting adults at that, and there was nothing wrong with a passionate kiss.

Tyler escorted her to her seat. Dinner was an experience in anticipation. Tyler trailed his foot up and down her calf, then had the nerve to reach over and trace the seam of her jeans with his fingertips and press against her already throbbing clit.

Not to be outdone, she gave it right back to him. He almost jumped out of his chair when she cupped his cock over his pants and squeezed. The others all grinned as if they knew what she and Tyler were doing.

They probably did. Her mind kept switching from desire to admiration when the servers brought out small cakes. Her eyes widened as she recognized these particular cakes.

"Not that we really have to worry about calories this week," she said, "but I should warn you, this particular dessert is about sixteen hundred calories on its own."

"How do you know that?" Sally asked before taking a bite.

"I work in catering, and there's only one company I know of that provides these. Delicious as they are, they're deadly to the waistline."

"That explains why Lou is so secretive about these desserts," Jared commented. "How long have you worked in catering?"

"Eight years in various positions within different hotels. Next week, I start at the Palace Hotel."

Peter whistled. "Quite an achievement."

"Yes." Becca ducked her head, looking at Tyler from beneath her lashes. The five-star hotel only hired the best. She didn't know what reaction she expected from Tyler, but he was grinning.

"Please tell us more about what you do," Jared said.

Becca talked for the next thirty minutes and was surprised how much she enjoyed talking about her work. Her mother never cared, and neither had Alan.

The conversation jumped from catering, to recipes to the best restaurants in San Francisco and before she knew it, they'd finished coffee and dessert. They all stood, said good night and left for their cabins.

Outside the lodge, Tyler pulled her to a stop. "I'll stop by your cabin in the morning to take you to the day's lecture."

"You don't have to do that."

"Yes, I do." He kissed her nose before trailing over her cheek to her ear. "Do you know how hard I am seeing you without a bra?"

"It's all your fault." She entwined her arms around his neck.

"How is that?" He nuzzled her neck.

"Those damn nipple danglers made them so sensitive. Even the shirt I'm wearing is driving me crazy."

He chuckled against her skin, sending delicious vibrations through her body.

"It's not funny." She tangled her fingers in his hair and tugged.

"How do you think I'm feeling?" His head lifted, and their gazes met. His eyes glittered with need. "I'm so hard that it'll take me days to get my dick to deflate. All because of your sweet, delicious, hot body." His hips met hers, and his desire was obvious.

"Come back to my cabin and let me see what I can do about that massive cock of yours."

His nostrils flared, and his gaze turned molten. He rested his forehead against hers, his hot breath brushing her skin.

"I'd take you up on that, but I have work to do."

Becca sighed as he pulled back. "So, you're going to leave me all worked up and alone."

"Yep." He placed her at arm's length. "Anticipation is part of foreplay. I'll see you in the morning." Releasing her, he turned and walked stiffly into the lodge.

She bit her lip to prevent herself from smiling. She wasn't the only one worked up and alone. The knowledge made her feel a little better as she made her way back to her cabin. Maybe she'd pull out a vibrator and have some solo fun.

Her clit throbbed. No, it wouldn't be fun without Tyler. Besides, she was so sensitive right now, she'd probably scream from just touching herself.

She sighed. Another night alone. This better not be for much longer.

I want Tyler in my bed.

***

The next morning, Becca was on her third cup of coffee when a knock sounded. She opened the cabin door to see Tyler standing there. He looked refreshed, well rested, and relaxed.

Damn him.

She'd spent the night tossing and turning in frustration. Becca wanted him in her bed, his hard body against hers, his arms around her. Reaching up, she curved her hand around his neck and covered his mouth with hers.

Coffee and mint and something else hit her taste buds. She tightened her arms around him as she continued the kiss. Maybe they could take this into the bedroom? No. She needed control. It was time for her to call the shots. She broke the kiss.

"Now that's a good morning," he said.

"A good morning would be me and you in my bed." Her dreams had been filled with him. Each time she woke, she was hot and sweaty. She almost climbed out of bed and pulled out a toy, but she didn't. Anticipation, he told her. Well, she was anticipating all right.

"Soon." He nudged her into the cabin. "I need to get you ready for today." He shut the door.

A tiny shiver worked its way up her spine. Excitement or apprehension, she couldn't tell. Probably a bit of both. She'd glanced at the lecture for today. Anal.

"Ah, Tyler." She crossed her arms over her belly.

"You're not backing out, are you?" He brushed a lock hair from her face, his fingers caressing her cheek.

"No, but..." She closed her eyes. How did she explain? Hell, she didn't quite understand it herself.

"Becca." His fingers curved around her jaw. "Open your eyes." Her gaze connected with his. "Fear is natural. Remember, you don't have to do anything you don't want to. You have your safe word."

"I know," she whispered.

"Good." He released her and walked into the bedroom.

Becca shifted from one foot to the other. It wasn't that she was afraid, or maybe she was. Damn, she hated being indecisive. Tyler emerged from the bedroom, concealing something in his hand. She really couldn't make it out.

"Come here, sweetheart." He held out his free hand.

"What do you have?" Part of her wanted to obey him, the other part wanted to run.

"I have something to make today a little more exciting." He stared at her, and the next thing she knew, she was standing in front of him without a clue how she got there. This man was a witch.

"I'm glad you're wearing shorts." His gaze traveled over her body. "How are your nipples today?" He tugged her with him as he moved backward and then sat in one of the chairs, with her standing in front of him.

"They're better."

"Good. Spread your legs for me, sweetheart."

She swallowed but did as he requested.

"Each day, we're going to build on what you've learned the previous day. Yesterday's lecture was about toys."

"I remember." What was he planning? He slid her shorts down her thighs.

"Are you wet, baby?" He slid his fingers inside her panties. What ever he had in his hand glided against her skin.

"Yes," she whispered.

"Good. I need you wet."

She was about to ask him why when something cool slipped into her pussy. Once Tyler removed his hand, she shifted from one foot to the other. Her skin was on fire from his touch. The object he'd pushed into her pussy shifted, but it wasn't a dildo or anything like that.

Tyler slid her shorts back into place and fastened them.

"What did you do?" she asked as her toes curled at the slight pressure of her clothing against her mound.

"I've placed two small pleasure balls deep inside your pussy." She shifted again. Not bad. She could handle this. "They will stay there throughout the lecture and lunch."

"That shouldn't be a problem." Confidence flowed through her voice.

"Oh?" He lifted his left hand. In it was a key fob. There were three buttons on it. His thumb pressed the first one.

She jumped. "Damn." The vibrations zinged through her body.

"Vibrating pleasure balls."

"You're not playing fair."

He smiled. "I never said I would."

The vibrations stopped and Becca took a deep breath, willing her pussy to stop twitching around the balls.

"This is a wireless remote, and it has three speeds. You'll never know when I'll turn it on." He slipped the fob into his pants pocket and took her hand. "Time for us to go."

Each step from her cabin across the compound to the lecture rooms was torture.

All right, she had to admit it was more arousal than torture, but every time those damn balls shifted within her, delicious sensations coursed through her body.

Halfway across the courtyard, Tyler turned on the balls, making her stumble. He caught her easily and held her until she could walk.

"Unless you want everyone to know about those balls, you better learn to control your reactions." He turned the device off.

Her pussy muscles tightened. "You think I can't?" How could she? She was on edge right now and that was probably what he wanted. He was playing her like a well-tuned instrument, and she didn't like it.

"We shall see." With his hand at her back, he guided her into the lecture room.

Becca sighed when she saw all the couples were there. She sat—carefully—on the mat, and Tyler dropped beside her.

Another couple walked into the room with several small boxes and what looked like a wedge.

"Hi, everyone. I'm Will, and this is my wife, Ella. Today, we're going to help you explore and understand anal sex."

Becca squeaked as Tyler turned the balls on.

"You have a question?" Will turned to her.

"No. Sorry." Becca glared at Tyler, but he wore an innocent expression. "*Something* startled me."

Will glanced at Tyler, then back to her, and nodded. "Ella will be my helper. We will show you how to prepare your partner for anal penetration. We'll also discuss the right way for penetration so both of you receive pleasure."

The vibrations stopped, and Becca almost sighed in relief.

This will be a loooong lecture.

***

Becca was never so glad to have a break between lunch and when Tyler would show up at her cabin. Using her foot, she pushed the porch swing into motion. She loved the back porch here, private and peaceful. She needed time to think after the lecture this morning because she wasn't sure about anything anymore.

I never realized how turned on I could be by watching another couple have sex. Anal sex at that. It helped that she hadn't been the only one affected. Several of the couples had climaxed, as had she. Only Tyler seemed unaffected. Either that or he had better control over his body than she thought.

He'd been hard. His cock pressed against her fabric-covered ass during the class and grew harder as things progressed. While the other couples climaxed while trying anal, she and Tyler hadn't. No, he reserved that for their private time. Instead, he turned those vibrating balls on at just the right time.

With a sigh, she closed her eyes and rested her head on the back of the swing cushion. Her left foot slipped, jarring her hip and a low moan escaped her. Tyler had told her she was to keep the balls inside her until he removed them.

Why didn't that command bother me?

Maybe because his dominance wasn't like her mother's. Tyler gave her a choice in their sexual play. A safe word. He didn't force anything on her, and she knew that by the time this week ended, she would be better in tune with her mind and body.

A sense of sadness flashed through her when she thought about leaving—which meant leaving Tyler behind.

Shaking her head, she shoved the thought away. She needed to concentrate on the here and now, because she suspected today would be much like yesterday with Tyler teasing her mercilessly.

A delicious shiver of anticipation shot through her body. Tyler told her he wouldn't take her ass today. She wasn't ready. But he would be using different toys on her ass.

Becca tried to remember what toys he'd put back in the cabinet yesterday. *Let's see, a box of plugs, a set of anal beads, an inflatable dildo...*

She trembled. Okay, that looked a little sinister, but after the class, she could handle the other toys.

She closed her eyes and wondered how much time she had before Tyler arrived. While her movement on the swing teased her pussy, it wasn't enough to push her over the edge.

"Yes, that's it, baby."

Startled, Becca opened her eyes. There was no one in the back with her, and she knew that voice. That was Maggie's voice.

Oh! Peter and Maggie's cabin was next to hers. But this was the first time she heard them.

"I love your tits." Peter's voice carried on the still air.

Damn, she should go back inside, but she was frozen with indecision.

"I know you do," Maggie commented.

"Ready, baby?"

"Yes. Fuck me. Fuck my ass."

Becca covered her mouth with her hand as she heard several grunts and sighs.

"How does that feel, baby?" Peter's voice sounded strained.

"Full, but so good. Between your cock in my ass and that vibrator in my pussy, I don't think there's another inch to be filled."

"There's still your mouth."

Becca's eyes widened, her hips shifted, and her slit began to pulse.

"We can do that later," Maggie said. "Please fuck me."

"Anytime, my love."

The next five minutes were filled with heavy breathing, the slapping of flesh against flesh, groans and moans. Occasionally, Maggie or Peter would talk, but not much.

"Oh god, yes. I'm almost there. Fuck me, darling. Fuck me hard. Turn the vibrator on high."

"I'm going to make you come, then come again and again." Peter's tone sounded possessive. "You're mine. *All* mine."

"Yes, I'm yours. Yes, that's it. I'm—" Maggie screamed.

That speared Becca into action. She jumped off the swing and high-tailed it back inside her cabin. She shut the doors quietly, her erratic pulse rushing in her ears. Thank goodness she couldn't hear the couple anymore.

"The cabins are soundproof."

Becca squealed and spun around to see Tyler standing by her bed, completely nude. "You scared me."

"Did you like what you heard?" He stalked over to her—there was no other word to describe his movement.

"I..." How could she answer that? "How long have you been here?"

"Long enough." His fingers toyed with the waistband of her shorts before slipping beneath and pushing them and her panties to the floor. "Did you want to touch yourself while you listened to Peter and Maggie fucking?"

She bit her lip. Arousal flowed through her, but she hadn't thought about caressing herself. She'd been concentrating on the couple next door.

"I can smell your sweet scent." Her T-shirt followed her shorts to the floor. His fingers slipped between her legs, and she shifted.

She wanted his touch, but while this was familiar, it was also new. All she could think about were the moans from the couple next door.

"Yes, you're wet. Excellent." His mouth captured hers as he thrust a finger into her.

Becca cried out into his mouth. His finger pressed against the balls still deep in her pussy. Her body was primed for whatever Tyler wanted.

"Did the vibrating balls bring you pleasure?" he asked after breaking the kiss.

"You know they did." She grasped his cock, enjoying the feel of his hardness beneath her fingers. "Is your cock needy?"

"Yes." He slowly removed the balls from her pussy, and a sigh escaped her.

While she was glad the balls were gone and no longer teasing her, her pussy felt empty. "What are we going to do today?"

"We'll build on yesterday. I thought we'd start with some nipple clamps, try out a few toys, and then play with your ass."

"Do I get to play with you?" She thought it was a little unfair that she received all the pleasure.

He grinned. "Yes. I can't wait for you to play with me." He turned and placed the black foam wedge on the bed.

She shifted from one foot to the other. Was he going to tease and torment her again today? She hoped not.

"On the bed, lie on your stomach, over the wedge."

Becca swallowed hard but followed his orders. Once she was in position, her ass was in the air and her shoulders on the bed. She wasn't sure what to do with her head.

"Here." Tyler helped her lift her head and put a pillow under it. "Better?"

"Yes." She turned her head, but she couldn't see Tyler.

Warm, masculine hands ran over her ass, and she squirmed.

"Easy." His lips followed his touch. Over her ass, then small kisses up her spine to the nape of her neck. "I'm glad your hair is up."

His touch disappeared. Then a soft *pop* caused her to shift and look over her shoulder. Not easy in the position she was in.

"What is in your hand?" She couldn't quite see.

"A bottle of lube."

Excitement and apprehension chased each other up her spine. Lube was a necessity in anal play. Becca closed her eyes and concentrated on relaxing her body.

Tyler massaged her ass.

"Ummm, that feels good," she said.

"Keep talking. Let me know how you feel or if something hurts." He paused and she heard the snap of gloves being put on.

He slipped his lubed-up finger between her ass cheeks. Becca fought not to squirm as she concentrated on relaxing all her muscles and sinking onto the wedge while Tyler probed and spread the lube. More lube, and then he pressed his fingers against her asshole.

"Breathe, sweetheart."

Air escaped her. When did she decide to hold her breath? His finger slipped into her ass, and she gasped. "Oh my." The two words were inadequate. Her ass tingled; it wasn't unpleasant, just different. More lube trickled down.

Another push of his finger and a slight pinch caused her nerves to quiver. His finger slid in and out as he added more lube. Heat filled her veins. When he pushed his finger all the way back in, her ass clenched around it.

"Okay?" he asked.

"Yes." Becca tried to gather her thoughts. "I can feel your finger inside me, stroking me; it's making me wet. It's different. I never expected it to feel this good."

More lube was added, and she felt new pressure against her ass. She sucked in a breath, willing herself to stay relaxed.

"Another finger, baby."

The pressure lessened. But her body was on fire. "I'm so hot, it's like there's liquid lava running through my veins."

"I'm sure." His lips caressed the small of her back while he stroked his fingers in and out of her ass. "So beautiful."

Her pussy clenched, and her clit tingled, causing her ass to tighten around his fingers.

"Ready for the next step?" He removed his fingers.

"I think so." Was that her breathless voice? New pressure was applied, and her fingers clenched the quilt.

"Exhale and press out, now."

"*Ahhh.*" Her body stiffened. It was a plug; how far had he gotten it in? Her ass burned a bit from the penetration. She panted as her body began adjusting to the plug. "More," she whispered.

Cool lube hit her overheated skin before another push of the plug. A moan left her lips.

"Okay, baby?" His breath caressed her ass cheeks.

"Yes. My ass is gripping the plug, and my pussy is clenching."

"Maybe this will help." He paused and slid two bare fingers into her wet pussy.

"Yes." She pressed down on his fingers. Becca wanted more.

She wanted everything he had to give her.

"That's it, baby." He stroked his fingers in her pussy. "I can feel the plug in your ass with my fingers. You're so damn hot and tight."

His words made the fire inside her burn hotter, brighter. "I feel full and yet..."

"Yet, what?"

Becca panted. How could she feel this way? It didn't make sense. "I want more. I want you to make me come."

"I can do that. I want you to think about how my cock is going to feel in your ass. Feel me sliding in and out, with my fingers in your pussy, my thumb on your clit. I'm going to take you to heights you've never known."

She couldn't catch her breath. Listening to his words heightened her arousal several notches. Her ass gripped the plug, and each time Tyler's fingers brushed against it, shafts of pleasure shot through her.

"You're close. Your pussy is gripping my fingers."

Becca was close. So close that it wouldn't take a lot push her over. "Yes. Take me. Take my ass, my pussy, make me come."

Tyler moaned. "When I fuck your ass, I'm going to make you come all over my fingers, but I won't stop there. I'll keep fucking you until you think you can't take anymore. But you can. I'll keep you so aroused and on edge that you won't know which way is up. Until you can't take any more, and you scream from pure pleasure as I spill myself inside your sweet tight ass."

He curved his fingers and hit her G-spot. Becca screamed as she began to climax. It seemed to go on for hours, but she knew it was bare minutes. She collapsed against the wedge, satisfied. Well satisfied. It was going to be hours before she could move.

Tyler removed his fingers and kissed the base of her spine. "We still have some time before dinner. What do you say we try the nipple danglers with the plug?"

Chapter Eleven

♥

Becca sat very carefully for dinner. Tyler had played with her body all afternoon. A thrill of excitement shot through her when he glanced over at her and winked. He'd given her about an hour without the butt plug, but before she dressed, he put it back in.

He'd told her he wanted her to get used to having it in her ass. Of course, he wasn't done. He put the nipple danglers on her for dinner. She couldn't wear a bra with them, and she didn't have a shirt that wouldn't show off her nipples. So unfair of him.

She glanced around the table. She wasn't the only one having problems. All the women squirmed in their seats, and their nipples showed through their shirts. Some wore nipple jewelry she could see beneath their shirts, and she couldn't be sure about the others.

Becca shifted in her seat. Dressing had been… difficult at best. With the butt plug in her ass and the nipple danglers on, every move she made caused arousal to shoot to her clit and pussy. She gasped as she shifted, and the butt plug shifted inside her.

"Okay?" Tyler asked softly.

"Fine." She fought to concentrate on the conversation going on around the table rather than the toys keeping her on edge, but it was a lost cause. She let the conversation float over her as she thought about the past few days with Tyler.

He'd opened her eyes to the sensual side she'd been burying. She knew she liked her sex with a little bit of kink, but this had shown her all kinds of new possibilities. Before it was just little more than the missionary position and not much else.

Now, toys had become a part of foreplay, talking to her partner about what felt good and what didn't. Keeping the lines of communication open, and now ass play. She was glad they still had a few days and nights to explore everything. She'd glanced at the schedule and realized there was still a lot for her to learn.

Tomorrow was *Beginners Bondage*, then the day after *Threesomes, Foursomes, and More*. Saturday was a free day, and Tyler had written in "special day." On Sunday, she'd leave for home.

Home. She felt at home *here* with Tyler on the ranch, but it was an illusion. One week, that was the deal, and she would keep her side of the bargain.

The bondage class didn't bother her too much, as she'd fantasized about being tied up. She had a feeling Tyler would love it. *Threesome, Foursome, and More* was a little disconcerting.

Oh, she'd fantasized about being with two men, but she couldn't imagine being with more than that.

Thoughts swirled through her head. Alternating heat surges rushed to her core and shivers of, well, almost apprehension, though for what, she had no clue. It wasn't until Maggie and Peter pushed back their chairs that Becca realized dinner was over. She looked down at her almost full plate. She'd been so lost in her thoughts that she didn't even eat.

"I had your refrigerator stocked during dinner," Tyler said, standing behind her chair. "Somehow, I had a feeling you wouldn't be eating much."

"The food is good. I'm just... distracted."

"Aroused and needy." He helped her from her chair and pulled her into his embrace. "I understand. I could barely keep my mind on food and the conversation." When he flexed his hips, his erection brushed against her.

Becca moaned, and her legs parted.

"Were you thinking about the plug in your ass?" He nipped her earlobe. "Or were you thinking about your hard nipples? Or maybe how my cock is going to feel in your wet pussy?"

Biting her lip, Becca dropped her forehead against his shoulder. If she was stronger, she'd throw him to the floor and have her way with him.

"Or maybe you were thinking that I'll use the triple suckers as I take you."

A tremor swept through her body. Oh, God, how would that feel? She couldn't wrap her mind around it.

"You like that idea," he said.

"Tyler, I..." She trembled as his fingers found the base of the plug through her clothing, and he wiggled it.

"So ready for me," he whispered as his right hand slipped around and down the front of her shorts. "So wet."

She gasped and squirmed as he plunged two fingers into her. "Anyone could come in." Luckily, they were still alone in the dining room.

"Who cares?" He stroked her pussy with one hand while the other played with the base of the plug. "Are you ready for what I want to do tonight?"

"Oh yes," she whispered. The afternoon had been fun, but she wanted Tyler inside her. She wanted to feel his hardness and give him pleasure.

"Ah, excuse me."

Becca jerked in Tyler's arms at Jared's voice. She stared over Tyler's shoulder to see Jared standing in the entrance of the dining room.

"Sorry, but there's a phone call for Becca."

"Me?" Who could be calling her here? No one knew she was here except—

"Said her name was Angie, and she's been trying to get you on your cell. I explained you didn't have your cell phone."

"It must be important. Angie would only bother me if it was." Becca felt a sense of loss when Tyler withdrew his hands.

"Come on, I'll show you where you can take the call." Jared motioned for her to precede him. She and Tyler followed Jared.

A million things ran through Becca's mind. Had her mother tried something? Or Alan? Nerves gathered in her belly as it tightened with dread.

Jared led them to an office. "Line two." He gestured to the desk and the phone.

"Thank you." Becca slipped away from Tyler's comforting arm and picked up the receiver. "Hey, Angie, what's up?"

***

Tyler stood outside his office to give Becca some privacy, but stayed close in case she needed him. Jared stood beside him.

"She's very responsive to you," Jared said. "She didn't even realize I was watching."

"Yes." Tyler grinned. "I have ways to keep her distracted."

"I bet." Jared laughed and clasped Tyler on the shoulder. "I really don't need you for the next few days."

"That's why I've been burning the midnight oil to make sure my work was done, and you wouldn't need me. I plan on spending my time with Becca."

"I figured." Jared ran his hand through his hair. "I'll announce tomorrow that dinner is now optional. All the couples tonight looked ready to explode."

"Yeah." Tyler watched Jared's face closely and noted the strain around Jared's eyes. "What is bothering you? Need to get laid?" Tyler was aware that Jared would go to a friend's house every so often to let off some steam.

From what Tyler understood, the friend had some very interesting parties.

Jared laughed. "Not yet, my friend. But there is something I'd like to ask."

"Go for it."

"If Becca decides to do a threesome, I'd like to be your third."

Tyler's eyes widened. This was a surprise.

Jared shook his head. "I know I don't participate, but the way she looks at you... I'm not a threat, and this way, maybe you'll both be comfortable."

Tyler saw the logic in Jared's words. "If she's willing, then I don't see a problem." Tyler didn't. Jared would follow his lead with Becca, and there wasn't another man he trusted more.

"Great." Jared turned and walked into his office across the hall as Becca hung up the phone. A frown marred her features.

"Problem?" Tyler crossed to her side.

"Not really. My new job moved my start to Monday morning instead of Tuesday. So I won't have an extra day to prepare now. Angie wanted to let me know." She smiled. "Am I to assume this is your office and not Jared's?"

"It is. What gave it away?"

"The horse pictures."

Tyler glanced at the wall that held the pictures. Figured she'd key on those rather than the other contents of the office.

"Where do you sleep?"

"Upstairs. The second and third floors are sealed off from everyone but Jared and me. That's our private domain."

She nodded. "Can we go back to my cabin and pick up where we were before we were interrupted?"

He laughed. Leave it to Becca to cut to the chase. "Race you."

"What?"

Laughter filled the air. He jogged backward. "You can run, can't you?" This was going to be fun.

She glared at him. "Yes, but—" She bit her bottom lip. So adorable.

"First one to the cabin gets to be in charge," he called over his shoulder as he sprinted for the front door. He knew she'd never be able to run with the plug in her ass and the danglers on her tits.

He leaped up the stairs at her cabin and turned to see her moving quickly across the courtyard, not quite running. Her breathing was labored when she joined him.

"Cheater."

Tyler grinned. "I want you to go into the bathroom and undress, then come back into the living room and sit on the sofa. Do not remove the danglers or the plug."

She stuck her tongue out at him before she walked into the cabin. Tyler followed but stayed in the bedroom as she went into the bathroom. He'd move some of his clothing over here tomorrow—along with anything else he might need for the next few days.

He headed to the cabinet and grabbed the lounger, massage oil, and a couple of vibrators. In the living room, he arranged everything, but his mind was on her phone call. She said her start date had been moved up.

His gut clenched. Their week was coming to an end in a few days. The thought made him sad, but she belonged in the city and he didn't. He heard the bathroom door open. Becca walked into the room in all her glory.

Without a word, she walked over, then hesitated when she saw the oil. He stared at her.

"Won't we get the cushions messed up?" Her voice was soft.

Leave her to think about that. "Just a second." He grabbed several towels out of the cabinet, then placed one on the sofa for her to sit on.

She perched on the edge. He flashed her a smile, laid two towels on the table and one on the floor.

"Be right back." Tyler went into the bathroom. He filled the basin with hot water, then grabbed a towel and placed it over the heated towel rack. When he returned, he found Becca staring at the items he'd set on the table.

He would treat her like a queen tonight. He placed the curved lounger and several pillows where he wanted them on the floor. "Are you ready for me, Becca?"

"Oh, yes."

"Then come here." She stood and made her way over to him. "So beautiful." He flicked the nipple danglers. To her credit, she didn't make a sound. He leaned over and covered one breast with his mouth.

She moaned as he suckled one nipple and then the other, making them even harder. He continued to play with her breasts as his fingers found the base of the butt plug. When he toyed with it, she stiffened.

Tyler bit her nipple playfully, and she groaned. Without hesitation, he pulled the plug from her ass. She cried out, and her body trembled. He tossed the plug onto the towel he'd placed on the floor.

He waited until she caught her breath before he removed the danglers. "Are you sore?"

She shifted from one foot to the other. "I don't think so."

"Good. Go lie down on the lounger and stretch out on your stomach."

Becca swallowed but followed his directions. He waited until she was in position before he stripped off his clothes. The curved lounger provided her head and hips support. Grabbing the first bottle from the table, he knelt on a pillow at her hips. He flipped open the lid and poured the oil into his palm before setting the bottle down.

He rubbed his hands together, then placed them on her shoulders. Becca jumped. "Easy," he murmured. "This is for you." He rubbed the oil into her shoulders and back, kneading the tight muscles.

She was wound up, and he didn't want that. He wanted her relaxed.

Tyler continued down her back, adding more oil as he needed until the scent of vanilla filled the air. At the base of her spine, he worked his hands outward.

"That feels so good," she whispered.

Avoiding her ass, he massaged the back of her thighs and her calves.

"*Ahhh.*"

He grinned as he massaged her lower legs, enjoying the feel of her muscles relaxing beneath his ministrations. After moving back up her body, he stood and headed to the bathroom, where he grabbed a washcloth from the counter and a towel off the warmer.

Perfect. He dunked the washcloth in the hot water, wrung it out, and returned to Becca. He ran the cloth over her skin to remove the oil, set the washcloth aside, and then grabbed the towel to dry her.

"Can you turn over, baby?"

Becca brought her knees up and managed to roll onto her back, watching him as he poured oil on his hands. He picked up her right foot. As he caressed it, and then the left foot, her eyes drifted shut. He massaged her until she was a boneless heap beneath his touch.

That's what I wanted. He'd avoided her ass and pussy...for now. He jumped up and rinsed the washcloth in the bathroom to warm it again, washed the oil off her skin, and dried her with the towel. Her eyes remained closed, her body totally relaxed against the lounger.

Good. He grabbed the tongue vibrator from the table before kneeling at her feet and setting the vibrator at his side. When he pressed his hands against the inside of her thighs, her legs parted easily. He picked up the tongue vibrator and put it on.

Tyler skimmed his hands up her legs, pulling her slightly toward him, and put her legs on his shoulders before he lowered his head. Becca bucked against his mouth as he licked her. He used the remote and turned on the tongue vibrator and licked her clit.

"Oh god. That's wicked."

His gaze captured hers, even as he continued to lick her. He thrust his tongue deep within her, and she arched against his mouth, her juices flowing around her mound. He twirled his tongue and toyed with her clit, then pushed three fingers into her pussy.

"Yesssss." Her head thrashed against the lounger.

He couldn't believe how wet she was. Her hands gripped his head, fingers tangling in his hair.

Time to take it up another notch. Tyler upped the vibrations and began moving his fingers.

"Oh, fuck yes." Her breathing came in short pants, her pussy contracting against his fingers. She was ready to climax.

Tyler placed the tongue vibrator directly on her clit and set it on high.

Becca stiffened as the climax rolled over her. Tyler rode the tremors all the way through and then brought her to her peak a second time. On the third time, she screamed, her entire body shaking with the force of her orgasm.

Tyler turned the vibrator off and lifted his head. Gently, he removed his fingers and lowered her legs onto the lounger.

Her hands fell limply to her side. He removed the vibrator, grabbed a fresh warm washcloth, and bathed her pussy.

"That feels so good." Her words were soft.

"I'm glad." Damn, this woman was so responsive. Even more than she'd been in college. Tossing the washcloth aside, he stood and picked her up, carrying her into the bedroom where he placed her on the bed.

She started to curl up. "Oh no, you don't." He climbed in beside her.

"Tyler?"

"The night is ours," he whispered before his mouth closed over hers.

Within minutes, she was squirming beneath him. It helped that he was caressing her breasts and her pussy.

"Take me, please. Fuck me."

Tonight, her words were sweet music to his ears. His cock needed her convulsing around him.

He needed it. Tucking her beneath him, her legs parted, welcoming him. The head of his dick brushed her entrance. "Ready?"

"Yes." Her legs curved around his waist.

He thrust, and her moan of pleasure made him grin before he captured her lips. She was his now. He retreated and then thrust. She'd already tightened around him. Neither of them would last long. They'd both been on edge for too long, especially him.

It only took four more strokes, and Becca climaxed. He smiled. They were going to have such fun tonight. He kept moving, his balls tightening, and he exploded. Tyler was still half hard when he pulled out of her luscious body. "Rest for a bit, then we'll continue."

***

Becca woke the next morning and stretched, wincing at her sore muscles.

She wasn't surprised by that. Reaching out her hand, she found a warm spot next to her. Opening her eyes, she wondered where Tyler was.

Damn, the man had stamina. He'd fucked her long and hard last night several times, and she didn't regret a second of it. Slipping out of bed, she padded to the bathroom. He wasn't in there. That was fine; she needed to clean up without help.

After taking a quick shower, she dressed and made her way into the kitchen. Tyler was sitting at the small table, and the smell of fresh coffee teased her senses.

"Good morning," he said with a smile.

"Morning." Embarrassment flooded her, and she wondered why. It wasn't as if she was a stranger to waking up with Tyler after a night of lovemaking. Somehow, this felt different than in college. Maybe she was different. She was beginning to lose her inhibitions, and it was because of Tyler.

Becca grabbed a mug and filled it before walking over to the table and sitting down. A sigh escaped her as her butt settled on the chair.

"Sore?"

"A little." He hadn't been that rough with her last night, but her ass hadn't been tormented like that before.

"Shall I take it easy on you today?" His gaze held humor even if he sounded serious.

"I'll be fine."

"Good." Tyler stood and crossed to her. "Finish your coffee. We have some time before breakfast. I intend to play with you today, however you want me to." He kissed her before leaving the room, the sound of his satisfied whistling filling the air.

Damn if her blood didn't heat and her pussy pulse. He could get her motors going so easily, not that it was a bad thing. She blew on her coffee and took several sips before dumping the rest of it. She didn't need coffee. She had Tyler.

***

Two hours later, Becca listened to Tyler's heartbeat as he cradled her against his chest. Her body still hummed from his lovemaking. She remembered this same feeling, but for a different reason.

"I can feel you smiling," he said. "What are you thinking?"

"Remember after finals that first year? We were both so wired from all the coffee."

"Remind me." His lips brushed the top of her head.

"We went back to your dorm room because your roommate had left, and they hadn't assigned you a new roomie yet." Her fingers traced circles on his abdomen. "We held each other for hours, laying there talking and kissing." She'd felt content in his arms then, just as she did now.

"I do remember." His fingers cupped her chin and tilted her head up. "One of my favorite memories." His lips caressed hers in a soft kiss.

"Mine too."

"What other memories do you have?"

"The day we went to the beach."

He laughed, and his chest rumbled beneath her. "It was fifty degrees, and we froze our asses off," he said.

"Yep." She couldn't help giggling, remembering the fog and wind. "You were so worried about me being cold, you took off your jacket and gave it to me."

"I was the one who caught a cold."

"You did, but I nursed you back to health."

"And you did a great job." His mouth found hers again. "You found a very sensual way to help me feel better."

"Then there was the time you helped me with my hotel hospitality project." Becca shifted her legs over his, brushing his cock.

"What else could I do? I wanted you to get an A."

"I don't think taking me to bed and fucking me silly was part of the plan." But, oh, how it worked. She'd awakened early the next morning with ideas.

"I enjoyed it, and it helped you relax."

She hit him in the shoulder.

"Ouch! What was that for?"

"Saying it helped me relax. I wasn't that tense." Her laughter filled the air. She hadn't felt this carefree in years, and she would enjoy every second of it.

"What about the time you helped me with my English homework?"

Becca rolled her eyes. "Please don't remind me. I think you shocked the teacher with your paper on *The Female Climax and Multiple Orgasms.*"

"I got a *B* on that paper."

"Then there was the paper on the sexual practices—"

His mouth covered hers, and there was no more talking. Becca didn't mind. Their time was coming to a close and she wanted to savor these new memories. She loved being with Tyler.

Chapter Twelve

♥

"Good morning, everyone. I'm Bart, and most of you know my wife, Liza. We're here to teach you the right way to experience basic bondage."

Becca shifted on the mat. Her body still hummed from Tyler's lovemaking. They'd had breakfast, then spent another hour in bed before arriving at their lecture at eleven.

"First off, you have to decide who is the Dominant or Top in the relationship."

"That's easy," Tyler whispered. "I'm the Dom."

Becca glared at him. "Who says?" She returned her attention to Bart.

"The Dom or Top is the one who wishes to be in control, and the submissive or bottom is the one who wants to be controlled, or to submit. You can choose one or the other, or even experiment. There is no reason you can't be both, and that's what we call a switch. And your labels can change as you feel like it."

Would Tyler let her take control of him? It wasn't like he was ordering her around all the time. Bart and Liza began putting various items on the mat in front of the couples.

"One of the first things," Liza started, "is that you have to fully trust your partner, if you want to enjoy bondage." Liza looked around the room. "If you don't trust the person one hundred percent to listen when you tell them to stop, you need to walk away."

Is that why I was never comfortable with other men?

But she trusted Tyler. Of course she did. They had a history together, and he'd done nothing since she arrived at the ranch but reinforce her trust in him. She wouldn't be here if she didn't.

"If you're the Dom," Bart said, "it's your responsibility to control the amount and type of stimulation the sub receives. As the sub, you must tell your Dom when things become too intense or if you're uncomfortable in any way."

"Always have a safe word," Liza commented. "Choose a word you wouldn't use in everyday conversation."

"Doms, when your sub says their safe word, you will stop what you're doing, check with your sub. In some cases, you might need to release them and sit down and talk about what happened." Bart rubbed Liza's back.

"It's very common for people to use *green*, *yellow*, and *red* as safe words," Liza said, leaning into Bart's embrace. "Like a stoplight. Green to keep going, yellow to slow down, and red to stop."

"Do you have a safe word?" Sally asked.

"Yes," Liza replied. "We use the stoplight system. You really do have to trust your partner. If you don't trust them to listen, then bondage is not for you."

"Bondage is not a game," Bart said. "Many people treat it that way, but there can be damaging consequences. Even if you try it today, you might not ever want to do it again, and that's okay. Everyone is different."

"Also," Liza said. "Using the right kind of rope is important if you use it for basic bondage. We're not going to get into anything more than bound hands and feet in this demonstration."

"We'll discuss which ropes are the best, the pitfalls and safety measures."

Bart took Liza's hand and helped her down onto the mat before he sat beside her. "Let's get started."

***

Three hours later when Becca walked into her cabin, Tyler was at her side. The second the door closed behind them, he backed her up against it and kissed her, hard. She kissed him right back, her fingers tangling in his hair.

The class today had been pure torture. Each demonstration heated her blood. She knew she was interested in bondage but never expected it to turn her on so much. There were many types of bondage, and they'd covered the basics: cuffs, restraints, and a little bit on rope play.

"Are you wet?" Tyler asked, his lips hovering above hers.

"Are you hard?" she shot back.

He reached up and pulled one of her hands from his hair, then pressed it between their bodies. His cock shifted when he molded her palm around it. Oh yeah, he was hard.

"I would have thought the classes wouldn't excite you so much." She squeezed him, enjoying the feel of his pulsing dick.

"This is the first time I've attended this class with someone who makes me hot"

Becca hit her head on the door as she jerked back in surprise. "Ouch."

"Easy." He rubbed the back of her head. "I don't ever want you to hurt. You mean too much to me." He kissed her, not the heated kisses she was used to, but tender, almost loving.

When he pulled back, it wasn't to kiss her neck. He locked gazes with her. "I want to be your everything, Becca. While you're here, of course. The last woman in my life was more interested in her career than in what I did for a living."

"Her loss is my gain." What woman would give him up?

But isn't that what I'm doing at the end of the week?

Yes, but they'd both gone into this with their eyes open. Falling in love wasn't an option and she would protect her heart at all costs. There was no other choice. They were from different worlds.

"I had lots of fantasies during class about restraining you and having you at my mercy." His breath brushed over her skin in a silky caress.

She bit her lip as her heart pounded. This was for her, and she wouldn't hold herself back. "I like the idea of being at your mercy."

His eyes blazed with desire. "Do you have a special fantasy?" He removed her hand from his groin.

"I want..." What would he think of her if she voiced her fantasy?

"Anything you want, sweetheart." He pressed his forehead against hers, their gazes holding each other. "Tell me."

Becca swallowed. "I've fantasized about my lover being in my bedroom while I'm unaware."

"Keep going."

Her tongue darted out and wet her lips. "He grabs me around my waist. I know it's him by the way he smells, so I'm not scared. He unbuttons my blouse and unhooks my bra. My breasts are on display for him. I start to squirm, and he turns me on my stomach and swats my ass, telling me to be still."

"Does he restrain you?"

"Yes, since I keep squirming. He's able to remove my pants and underwear and then ties me spread-eagle." Damn, this was arousing her.

"Then what?" The fire in Tyler's eyes blazed hotter.

"He teases me, torments me, all the while telling me how much he's going to enjoy fucking me every way he can."

"Sounds like fun." Straightening, Tyler released her hands. "Go into the bedroom and putter around."

Her pulse raced as she stepped around Tyler.

"Oh, and Becca?" She looked over her shoulder at him. "Safe word is *tomato* or *red*."

Her breath caught in her throat, but she nodded.

This will be one interesting afternoon.

Anticipation flowed through her veins. Inside the bedroom, she walked over to the French doors and stared out.

She couldn't hear anything from the other room. Had she made a mistake in telling him? No, she hadn't. He asked, and Tyler was the most open man about sex that she'd ever known. He wasn't one to run from one little fantasy. She had others that were more graphic.

Strong hands captured her arms and pulled them behind her back. One hand encased her wrists. "Hello, love."

Excitement snaked through her body. She hadn't even heard him enter the room. "Let me go!" She tugged, trying to free her arms.

"Not going to happen."

Fabric looped around her wrists and tightened.

"What are you doing?" She made sure her voice had a wobble in it, even though she was more excited than afraid.

"What do you think?" The fabric was tight, but not so much to cut off her circulation. His chest pressed against her back, and he reached around and began lifting her T-shirt.

Becca tried to sidestep him, but his hands captured her waist, stilling her movements. "Be still, woman. We're going to do this my way." Keeping one arm around her waist, he pushed her shirt up and over her head, but it was trapped around her shoulders. "I didn't think this through."

"Please stop," she cried. Tyler wouldn't, not unless she said her safe word, and right now she saw no reason to.

"Nope. Stay there." He let her go.

She waited and then realized she needed to be more proactive. She turned and was going to run until she saw Tyler standing in the doorway with scissors in his hand. "Bad girl." He stalked over to her. "Is it okay if I cut away your shirt and bra?"

Becca nodded. She could buy more.

He cut the shirt and bra straps and then flung the ruined clothing across the room and put the scissors on the nightstand.

"How dare you!" She tried to stomp his toes, but he danced back before she could make contact. This was pleasurable with someone she trusted.

"Oh darling, we're going to have so much fun." He spun her around, and his hand came down on her ass.

"Ouch." Not that it really hurt, but her blood heated in her veins.

"That's just a taste." He turned her back to face him. "Let me tell you how this is going to go." His raised his hands, and his palms covered her breasts. "You're mine for the afternoon, and maybe even tonight."

"Please," she whispered softly as her pussy clenched.

"I will please you." He pinched her nipples, and a moan escaped her lips. "Her body trembled with excitement.

"Such a good girl." He lifted his hands, and her world went dark.

She gasped, "What are you..." as she stumbled against Tyler.

"Easy." His hands rested on her shoulders. "It's just a blindfold."

Becca bit her lip. Tyler was taking her fantasy further than she expected. Her breathing sped up. His fingers trailed over her collarbone to the top of her breasts.

"So pretty." His fingers kept moving until they slipped beneath the waistband of her shorts. She shifted from one foot to the other.

"I said be still." He hit her ass. Unable to help herself, she wiggled again.

"You're making me think you want to be punished."

Becca stopped moving. Cool air touched her thighs as he stripped her shorts and underwear down her legs in one quick motion.

"No, please." She tried to keep in character, even though she was wet for him.

"Oh, you *will* please me." He scooped her into his arms and she cried out as he tossed her onto the mattress.

She could barely breathe. Tyler kept surprising her.

The mattress dipped and he didn't give her a chance to react. He gathered her wrists and pulled them over her head.

She opened her mouth, trying to draw more air into her lungs. When she felt him straighten she tugged her arms, but he'd restrained her to the bed.

How did he manage that? She tugged again.

"You can't get away." His breath flowed over her face.

He shifted and then was gone. Becca strained to hear him. Then his fingers encircled her left ankle.

"No." She half-heartedly kicked out.

"Oh, yes." He pulled her leg out and restrained it before doing the same with the right one. Cool air hit her pussy and ass. She was open to him for whatever he wanted to do. A shiver washed through her.

"I set all of this up days ago." She heard him moving around. "I've been watching you. I hid the restraints under your mattress until you were ready for me." His calm, even voice floated over her, soothing her nerves. "Now that you're at my mercy, what shall I do?"

Becca bit her lip, listening to him prowl around the room. What was he up to? She hated not being able to see.

"What do we have here?" His voice held a note of surprise. "My little girlfriend is a closet slut, is she?"

She didn't hesitate. "*Tomato.*"

"Are you hurting?" Tyler checked the restraints around her arms and legs.

"No." She took a breath. "Please don't call me a slut. I hate that word."

"Sorry, I won't use that word again. Anything else that might trigger you?"

"I'm good, thank you." Her belly fluttered. He'd listened to her and stopped to check in with her.

"All right then. Where was I? Oh, yes. All these lovely toys. We're going to have fun this afternoon."

His voice floated across the room, and she realized he was at the cabinet, acting like he'd never seen it before. What was he picking out? She turned her head, hoping to lift an edge of the blindfold, but it didn't move.

He spoke from right next to her. "Your body looks flushed. Are you hot?" When had he moved back to the bed?

"Let's see if I can cool you down a bit. I can't have you overheating as we play."

Something clinked, and she tried to place it. Cold touched her skin. Her back arched as much as it could in the restraints. The cold traveled over her breasts to her nipple, making it stiffen.

"*Ahhh!*"

"Very good." He trailed what her mind finally recognized was an ice cube between her breasts to her belly.

When did he get that? Probably when she couldn't hear him; this man was tricky.

The ice made her shiver, but it did cool her rather rapidly. Another *clink*, and she sucked in a breath, waiting for what he was going to do with this one. He circled her navel with it, then moved lower.

He wouldn't dare!

But he did. He maneuvered the ice over her mound and along her slit. She shifted her hips to get away from the cold.

"You can't seem to hold still, can you?" There was laughter in his voice.

"I'll get even." If it was the last thing she did, she'd get even with Tyler. He was taking the fantasy so much further than she ever dreamed about.

"I'm looking forward to it." He pushed the piece of ice into her pussy.

"Son of a—" Becca tried to twist away from him and the cold, but she couldn't. So cold, but so hot at the same time.

"Now that I've cooled you down a bit…"

She strained to hear anything because she wanted to know what he was going to do next as water dripped out of her onto the bed.

"Remove the blindfold," she demanded.

"Not a chance." His cool fingers pinched her nipple. "Nice, big nipples." He tugged at her right one, and then her left.

She took a breath when his touch disappeared, only to lose it when he snapped the first clamp on her nipple, and quickly did the second one. These were different than the ones they played with before. There was something resting between her breasts. Something metal. What was he planning?

The metal was lifted and... "Damn!" she cried out as he tugged.

"Nipple chain," he commented. His lips pressed against her skin as his fingers covered her mound.

She twisted, trying to get away, but it was impossible.

"Little squirmer." He slid two fingers into her pussy. "So wet, so hot." His breath brushed her skin before his cool cheek laid against her tummy.

"You're so wide open for me. That's why I like these restraints. I can spread your legs far apart and see all your secrets." He shifted his fingers within her. "I'm enjoying how your pussy is sucking at my fingers."

A third digit joined the other two, and Becca moaned as he stretched her.

"So pretty. Your pussy is flushed, and your clit is begging for attention. Shall I give it some?"

She couldn't answer. Her mind was grappling with the tingling in her nipples, and his fingers in her pussy.

Something cool and round pressed against her clit. An egg? A vibrating bullet?

She sucked in a deep breath, anticipating anything.

"*My* pussy," he whispered, lifting his head from her stomach. The toy on her clit shifted and then returned with more pressure than before. Her clit began to pulse.

She wasn't going to be able to take much more. Her entire body began to tingle, her climax close.

"My beautiful one, are you ready?"

She opened her mouth to tell him no, but no words came out.

He turned on the toy and vibrations attacked her clit. She tugged at the restraints, trying to close her legs, anything to stop this torment.

"How long can you last?"

Those words sent a shiver of arousal from her toes all the way to the top of her head. The mattress beneath her shifted as he began thrusting his fingers in and out of her pussy.

How was that damn toy on her clit staying in place? Her nipples throbbed in time with the pulsing toy.

"You're going to come when I tell you to, baby. You see, the bullet I have on your clit is one that I control, so let's see if I can make you come on demand."

Come on demand? What does he mean by that?

His fingers stroked her, but now at a leisurely pace, not too fast, not too slow. The bullet was on low, at least she thought it was, but it didn't stop her body from reacting to it. Yet it wasn't enough to throw her over the edge.

Damn, he was serious when he said he planned to torture her all afternoon.

The speed of the bullet increased, and Becca fought for control. Each time her body took a step closer to her climax, he'd turn the bullet down and stop stroking her, then start all over again.

Time after time he tormented her. He was playing her like a finely tuned piano. Sweat beaded on her body; her pussy contracted around his fingers, and her head thrashed against the pillow.

"Are you getting close again, baby?"

She couldn't take it. "Please. I need to come."

"Of course, you do." The bullet vibrations increased, and she began to pant.

Her body bucked, her pussy fluttered, her belly tightened, and her toes curled. "Tyler."

"That's it, baby."

The toy was turned higher. She couldn't believe it wasn't on high already. Tyler's fingers plunged harder into her pussy, and then he curved two of his fingers. "Come now, my love." He pressed against her G-spot and tugged the chain on the nipple clamps.

Becca screamed as her body exploded. From nipples to her clit, every nerve ending blew at once. She was flying apart and loving every second of it.

***

Tyler studied Becca's face as she climaxed. God, she was beautiful. Her pussy tightened and released around his fingers. When he finally turned the bullet vibrator off and let it rest against her clit, Becca lay limp against the sheets, her chest rising and falling rapidly.

He slipped his fingers from her wet core and then removed the bullet. Setting them aside, he slid up her body. When he removed the clamps and bloodflow fully returned to her nipples, it was going to send sensations through her body. Tyler moved into position, took the clamp off, and lowered his head, his mouth enveloping the torrid tip of her nipple. She moaned and arched her back. He waited until she fell back against the bed before doing the same with the second one.

When Becca settled down against the mattress, he stood and stared at her flushed body. She couldn't be more beautiful than she was at that moment, enjoying the deep, rosy glow of her orgasm.

He grinned. There would be more of those climaxes. He strode into the bathroom with the toys and cleaned them up. Tyler soaked a washcloth under warm water, then grabbed a towel. Back in the bedroom, he knelt on the bed and began wiping the sweat from Becca's body.

"*Hmmm*, that's nice," she murmured.

He dried her off, then tossed the towel and washcloth back into the bathroom. He was ready for more.

"Are you going to release me?"

"I'm not done yet." He checked her hands and feet; they were warm, and he didn't see any chafing or signs the bindings were cutting off her circulation. "Remember, I said you were to be mine all afternoon."

She groaned.

Maneuvering around the bed, he picked up the lube he'd set out earlier. Time for a little ass play.

***

Becca fought against the urge to squirm as she waited for Tyler. He had said all afternoon, but she'd thought he was just kidding. Apparently not.

She jumped when his cool wet finger touched her ass.

Oh, brother. Was she ready for this? His finger slid in and then out. More lube, then back in. This continued until she writhed in pleasure. A pause and then pressure. Fighting her instincts to push back, she took a deep breath and relaxed.

"Good, baby." The toy slipped into her ass. "I've put in a medium butt plug, and it will stay there for the rest of the day."

Becca wet her lips. Already, her body temperature was rising.

"Now, let's see what else I can find to play with."

She groaned and tugged at the restraints. She was at his mercy, and damned if she wasn't getting wet.

This was going to be a long afternoon.

Chapter Thirteen

♥

Becca woke the next morning in Tyler's arms. He'd spent the night. She laid there for a moment, enjoying the warmth of his chest against her back. His coarse chest hair brushed against her skin, and his breath teased her nerves.

"Good morning." His lips nuzzled her neck.

"Morning." She closed her eyes and let herself feel him. His cock pressed against her ass. "I don't know how you can be hard this morning." They'd played all afternoon. He'd only released her for dinner.

Hell, they made love most of the night, and now he was erect again. That man had more stamina than she did. His hand brushed her breasts, and her nipples rose in attention, her body so attuned to him. How could he affect her like this? Her libido had never been this active before.

"I'm in a state of perpetual erection around you." He eased her onto her back and captured her lips in a soul-deep kiss, one that curled her toes and made the blood sing in her veins. As she reached from him, he broke the kiss and rolled out of bed.

"Shower and breakfast are how we're going to start today."

Becca wanted to coax him back into bed but thought better of it. She stood and winced.

"Sore?" He was at her side in a second.

"A bit." She put her arms over her head and stretched. Muscles protested. "Someone kept me tied up and had his way with me yesterday. A lot."

"Yes, but he also massaged away the aches and pain." Tyler put his arm around her waist and guided her into the bathroom.

"True. And I really appreciated it."

"You'll appreciate a hot shower even more." He slapped her ass, and she laughed.

But her laughter dimmed, Sunday would be here soon.

She was going to miss Tyler.

***

An hour later, Becca glanced at Tyler from behind her coffee mug while they sat at the table in her cabin. Their breakfast dishes were empty, and they were enjoying another cup of coffee before they attended today's lecture. Their time was coming to an end.

She was also beginning to realize that her feelings for Tyler were more than superficial.

"I can't remember what the lecture is today."

He grinned. "I think I'll let it be a surprise."

"I'd rather know."

"Nope." He stood and picked up their empty plates. "Come on. I need to get you ready."

Becca bit her lower lip. *Get me ready? What does he plan on doing to me?*

After putting her mug in the sink, she followed him into the bedroom. This explained why he would only let her put on a robe after their shower.

She kept her gaze on him as he walked over to the cabinet and pulled out lube, a butt plug, and an unusual looking piece of fabric. She swallowed, hard.

"Nothing too strenuous today," he said, placing the items on the nightstand.

"That's what you say."

"Come here." He held out his hand. With a sigh, she walked over to him. He untied her robe and slipped it off her body. "Bend over and place your hands on the mattress."

Damn if her pussy didn't get wet at his words, and every neuron in her brain fired with excitement.

"Such a nice ass." He caressed the globes. "Tomorrow, I'm going to enjoy making it blush. Would you enjoy that?"

"Oh yes." His words just made her hotter.

"Good." A well-lubed finger slid into her ass, followed by a second one. When he twisted them, she flexed her ass against his fingers. "So ready for me." His fingers withdrew, then the tip of something hard nudged against her ass.

Becca took a deep breath as he worked the plug into her ass. This one was big, and when the plug was finally seated, she was positive there wasn't room in her ass for anything else. She felt full, and delicious shivers of arousal danced over her pussy.

"You can straighten up now."

She did, and a moan escaped her lips. "Damn, that's big."

"Think about how big my cock will feel sliding into your ass." He turned and picked up garment he'd taken out. "Your panties for the day."

Becca frowned.

"Trust me." He knelt in front of her, holding the panties out. "Step into them."

You only live once. She stepped into what he called panties. Tyler slid them up over her legs, thighs, until the elastic settled on her waist. But they felt odd.

"Widen your stance, please."

She did, and Tyler knelt again. He adjusted the fabric in the back, and she couldn't help but squirm when he touched the butt plug. His fingers brushed her mound next, and her hips flexed. But he didn't take the hint to touch her. Instead, he fiddled with the front of the panties.

Becca glanced down, but he blocked her view. She had no idea what he was doing, but something slid inside her. His finger brushed her clit before the fabric settled over her skin, and he stood.

"Now you can get dressed. Maybe an oversized shirt, since you won't be wearing a bra."

"All right." She took a step and... "What have you done?" She took another step and found that each time she moved, something hard moved in her pussy, brushed her clit, and with the plug in her ass, her arousal went from ten to one thousand.

"A small dildo and clit teaser to keep you on edge."

Becca placed her hands on her hips and glared at him. "Well, if I have to wear these toys it's only fair that you wear something too." Carefully, she made her way over to the toy cabinet. What could she do to him?

Heat surrounded her as Tyler came up behind her. "This is for your pleasure, not mine."

She spotted the cock harness and held it. "Wear this for me."

He groaned. "What? You think I'm not going to stay hard?"

Becca giggled. "You'll stay hard, all right, especially with that on." She turned, and caressed his rock-hard cock. Kneeling, she slipped the cock harness on him, and then encased his balls in the fabric, making sure it wasn't too tight. She licked his cock before standing. "I wonder which one of us will come first."

"You will." He sauntered across the room to his clothes.

"Oh, really?" Becca pulled on a light pair of shorts and a large shirt. She looked down, happy that it somewhat disguised she wasn't wearing a bra.

"You will climax before me," he declared.

"Want to bet?" *Where did that come from?* She continued to surprise herself.

Tyler stared at her, then a sexy grin spread across his face as his eyes gleamed. "Whichever one of us orgasms first, the other gets to pick what they're going to do to that person."

"Within limits," she added.

"Always within limits."

"Deal."

His grin widened. "Never bet unless you're sure you'll win."

"I will win," she declared.

His laughter filled the room as he finished dressing.

***

"You're cheating," Becca whispered to Tyler thirty minutes later as they sat on the mat in the lecture. This man was the devil himself. He'd put a vibrating butt plug inside her, and he kept turning it on—along with the clit teaser in her panties.

"I told you: Never bet unless you're going to win." His smug grin made her want to slap him.

She squirmed. When she made the bet, she was positive she could hold her orgasms off, but now she wasn't so sure.

Especially when he kept flipping the vibrations on and off.

"Sorry I'm late," Jared said, as he walked into the room and sat on the mat in front of them. The Carpenters and Watsons were both in class with them today. "Today's lecture is about ménages, foursomes, and more."

Oh hell. That's right. This was the last lecture. Becca glared at Tyler, but he ignored her.

"There is nothing wrong with wanting to add a third, or fourth, or more to your relationship." Jared's gaze went to each couple. "What you need to remember is that, as a couple, you decide together how many people you want to add to your sex life. It can be a one-time thing, more than once, only for sex, or for a more lasting relationship."

Becca almost jumped off the mat when Tyler turned on the butt plug again.

Damn that man! She would have her revenge on him.

***

"So, do you want to add a third?" Tyler asked her when they returned to the cabin.

Becca turned and poked a finger into his chest. "Right now, I want to kill you. Oh!" She hopped back as he turned the toys on again.

"Damn it, Tyler." Her knees were already trembling from the force of her first climax as they walked back to the cabin, and now, another one was building.

"I told you you'd come first." He gathered her into his arms and kissed her while tremors of pleasure washed through her body.

"Okay, fine. You won the bet. Turn them off, please?"

When the toys stilled, Becca sighed. Now, maybe, she could keep her control in place. "I need a drink." She walked into the kitchen and pulled a soda out of the fridge.

Tyler joined her when she sat at the table. "You mentioned to me that you'd thought about a ménage."

She nodded, unsure of exactly what she wanted. So much had changed in her this week. It was almost as if she didn't know herself anymore. Tyler brought out her sensual side, a side she'd kept hidden from the world.

"Are you willing to try one?" he asked.

"I don't know." That was the truth after the lecture. So much to decide. "Are you thinking of adding a man or woman?"

"Man." His answer was quick and firm.

She shifted on her chair. She wasn't sure if she could picture herself with any of the other couples there. "You obviously have someone in mind."

"Yes. I don't feel comfortable with a man who is in a committed relationship, and Jared has volunteered his services."

Becca almost fell to the floor. "But you said you don't get involved with guests."

"We don't. You're a special case." He reached across the table and took her hand.

"When Jared found out I'd come to the ranch alone—"

"Remember, he and I talked. He was fine with me being your partner. We've never gotten involved with anyone at the ranch. You are different."

How did she really feel about this? Yes, it was a fantasy, but Jared was intense, and she didn't know him.

Trust. That's what it came down to. If Tyler trusted Jared, then she could too.

"Would Jared...ummm..." She couldn't get the words out, but why? She hadn't had a problem talking with Tyler since the beginning of the week.

"Up to you." Tyler's fingers tightened around hers. "He can fuck you, or you can suck him off. It's your choice, Becca. I know you wanted to try it, and I want you to have this chance."

"I need to think about it." This was a big step for her. She shivered.

"Fair enough. I'll need an answer tonight, so I can get everything arranged."

"Not a problem."

He nodded. "Are you ready for your afternoon lesson?" He released her fingers.

The gleam in his eyes told her she was in for another long afternoon. "Bring it on." She wasn't going to shy away.

Chapter Fourteen

♥

Tyler watched Becca's face as they discussed the possibility of a ménage. He didn't know if she realized it, but her reactions revealed what he interpreted as arousal—adorably flushed cheeks and quickened breathing. Even more so when he mentioned Jared's name.

"Since I won the bet," he reminded her, "you have to pay up."

"I still say you cheated."

"I used all the weapons I had available." Thankfully, she hadn't picked the vibration cock and ball pouch. He'd barely held it together today. Standing, he held out his hand.

"Very effective weapons." She placed her hand in his. Tyler led her through the bedroom and into the bathroom. Once he released her, he turned on the water to fill the tub. "Undress and I'll remove the toys."

"Thank goodness." She stripped, and he removed the toys. Her body shuddered as he did so. She was so damn responsive.

Tyler dropped the toys into the sink to be cleaned later. He checked the water level in the tub, and added several drops scented bath oil into the water. "Take a nice relaxing bath while I prepare the bedroom."

"Why don't I like the sound of that?" Becca climbed into the tub, sighing as she sank into the hot water.

"I've used a vanilla rose oil in the water, so you'll want to rinse off once you're done soaking."

"Okay."

"Also, think about everything you've learned over the week, because we're going to cover it this afternoon." He turned and left. This afternoon would be a test of his endurance, but he didn't mind at all.

Until Becca gave him the green light on the ménage, he couldn't make any plans for tomorrow. Although he'd already reserved one of the special cabins for them. They had several of them on the ranch for guest use.

Glancing around the bedroom, Tyler realized it wasn't big enough. He wanted to give her a taste of what tomorrow would be like. In the living room, he began moving furniture out of the way.

Once that was done, he grabbed the lounger from the corner of the bedroom and positioned it where he wanted it. Then he moved one of the small tables over and tested his reach.

Perfect. Back in the bedroom, he pulled out all the toys he wanted to use.

Tyler filled two bowls with hot water, another bowl with ice, and carried them to the table. He grabbed several towels and washcloths out of the linen closet, then at the last minute, opened the French doors.

It was a nice day, and the fresh air would be good for both of them. Tyler surveyed everything. Yep, he had all he needed, except for Becca. In the bedroom, he stripped but left the pouch on. Not that he needed it, but it reminded him to keep his control. He couldn't stop running his hand over his dick.

A feminine sigh floated to him. "I've never seen a man stroke himself before."

"Maybe I can rectify that, later." He crossed to her. She was wearing a robe again. "May I braid your hair?"

Becca gave him a puzzled look. "Sure."

He snagged a brush and one of her hair ties off the counter. She watched him from the bedroom door. He grabbed several pillows off the bed and tossed them on the floor. "Come over here and sit on the pillows," he said as he lowered himself onto the mattress.

"I think you need attention, first." She knelt on the pillows.

His cock jumped at her nearness. Control. He had to have control. "Later."

"That's always your answer."

He lifted his hands to her shoulders. "Sit."

"I'm not a dog," she huffed before she flopped down on her butt on the pillows.

"No, you're not. You're a beautiful woman." Tyler pulled the brush through her hair. It felt like silk against his fingers. Within minutes, he had her hair braided. "All done."

She lifted her hand and ran it down the length of her hair. "Where did you learn to do that?" she asked, rising onto her knees and turning to face him.

Tyler closed his eyes so she wouldn't see the pain he was sure was reflected in them. "I used to do it for my mom when she got too sick to do it for herself."

"Oh, Tyler." Her lips brushed over his. "I'm glad you were there for her."

"So am I." They'd talked the other night, and he'd explained his mother had died from cancer several years ago. Now he felt at peace. He helped her rise from the floor.

He untied the robe's belt and stripped it from her before taking her hand and leading her into the living room. She gasped when she saw what he'd done.

"You can use your safe word—*tomato*—to stop every-thing, or *green*, *yellow*, and *red*. From this moment for-ward, I'm your Dom, and you follow my orders."

She opened her mouth and then shut it and nodded sharply.

"Good girl. Use your safe words as you need them."

"I understand."

"Go over to the lounger and lay on your stomach."

He kept his gaze on her as she walked over to it, but her focus was on the toys on the table. He watched her tremble slightly, and he didn't know if it was from excitement or fear. He waited until she positioned herself on the lounger before he moved.

Tyler knelt next to the lounger and picked up the bottle of massage oil. Pouring a generous amount onto his palm, he rubbed his hands together, then started the massage. He gave her a full body massage, front and back. When he finished, he made sure she was back on her stomach and connected the restraints to her wrists and ankles.

"You are sneaky," she said softly.

"Yes. I love this lounger for that reason. It has built in restraints, but I can also have you in different positions."

He rubbed her ass with one hand while he reached over and picked up the rabbit fur flogger.

It was a beginner flogger and would warm Becca up nicely. Removing his left hand from her ass, he brought the flogger down on her right ass cheek.

A cry of surprise left her lips as he smacked her left ass cheek. He paused and ran his hand over her ass. "How are we doing?"

"Green." Her voice sounded strained, and he only used the flogger twice.

He gave her ass several more swats before stopping to caress her skin. She squirmed. Her skin was warm to his touch, her body flushed, and her breathing rapid.

Time to move on.

Tyler set the flogger aside and picked up the lube. He dribbled it down her ass crack.

"Cold," she murmured.

Using his finger, he rubbed the lube around and added more. When his finger was nice and wet, he slipped it into her ass.

Becca groaned.

"Tell me what you're feeling," he ordered.

"Hot. My skin is tingling. My ass feels like it's on fire, and your finger is teasing me."

"Is that all?" He slid a second finger in.

"My pussy is wet, and my nipples are hard." Her breath was coming in little pants now.

Satisfaction flowed through him. "That's what I want." He pushed a third finger into her ass, and her hole tightened around him. "Don't come," he ordered, smacking her ass with his hand.

"You love to tease." She shifted in the restraints.

"I do." He slapped her ass again before picking up the butt plug he wanted and lubing it up. Tyler removed his fingers and teased her ass with the tip of the plug before slipping it in.

"Ohhhh." Her breath whooshed out.

"Yes, this is a bigger plug." Tyler slid it in and then out, letting her get used to the width of the plug. With his free hand he slid his finger into her pussy. She was dripping wet. A grin spread over his lips. He slid two fingers into her pussy as he moved the plug in her ass.

"Oh, God." She tried to press her pelvis against his fingers, but because of the way the lounger was curved, she couldn't press down.

He continued to caress her pussy and play with her ass until she was constantly moving on the lounger. Tyler pushed the plug completely into her ass.

"I need to come," she cried out.

"You will not." Lord, she was stunning. Her body was a beautiful rosy color, her breathing erratic, and he almost couldn't wait. He let her adjust to the plug in her ass as he fingered her pussy with three fingers.

Her moans increased along with the flushing of her body. It was time. He replaced his fingers with his cock.

Becca screamed as he thrust into her, filling her on the first stroke. Tyler lightly massaged her back as he held still, letting her adjust to his invasion. He could feel the plug in her ass as it twitched.

"Baby?"

"Yellow. Let me catch my breath."

"Of course." He kept stroking her hot skin, as he watched her regulate her breathing. She was so perfect. She hadn't used her safe word, and in a way, he'd expected her to. This was as close as he could get to having two cocks inside her. Well, he could use a double-headed dildo, or a strap-on, but he liked being in her pussy.

"I'm better now."

"I'm going to continue then." He withdrew and slowly slid in again. Her little moans of pleasure ramped up his desire.

"You're still wearing the harness, aren't you?" Her question came in short bursts.

"Yes. It will keep me hard and allow me to fuck you for a longer period of time."

"But..." Her pussy tightened around him as he sank into her warm depths. "I don't know..." Her head turned from side to side on the pillow.

Tyler grinned. Time to raise the stakes a bit. He reached over and hit the button on the remote.

"You're going to kill me," she yelled as the butt plug came to life.

"Never. We're just beginning."

She groaned, and her body sagged a bit. Tyler grabbed the remote and placed it at the small of her back so he could reach it easily. "Time for you to really feel what it will be like having two cocks in you. One in your ass and one in your pussy, bringing you pleasure over and over again." His heart pounded. It was time to show her all the gratification she could take.

Bracing his hands on the curve of the lounger near her waist, he began to fuck her hard and fast. Her pussy tightened around him on each thrust. With care, he balanced himself on one hand and turned the butt plug up a step.

"Yes. Oh, yes, Tyler! Take me. I'm yours."

Her words were sweet magic to his ears. He maintained his pace, watching her carefully. This was for her enjoyment, to show her how two men loving her could be sensual and fulfilling. Her body trembled.

Yes, it was time. He pushed the last button on the remote. "Come for me, baby." He pulled out to the tip of his dick and then thrust all the way in.

Becca cried out as her body spasmed around him. His balls tightened, but he willed his climax back. He rode out the tremors shaking her body, then turned off the butt plug and withdrew from her ass.

She lay there panting and moaned softly when he removed the butt plug. He picked up a washcloth and dipped it in the warm water.

"That feels good," she murmured as he bathed the sweat, lube, and her climax from her body.

"I'm glad." He finished and dried her skin so she wouldn't get chilled, and then he removed the restraints. She laid there not moving. "Turn over."

Becca glared at him but rolled onto her back. He helped her adjust on the lounger since he'd put in the center piece they hadn't used before, making the dip in the middle level. Then he put the restraints back on her and made sure they were tight but not too tight.

Her legs dangled on either side of the lounger, keeping her pussy open to him and her back near the headrest. "Are you in pain anywhere?"

She shook her head. He wasn't convinced. "Baby," he said softly, waiting until her gaze locked with his. "I need words. I need to make sure you aren't hurting and are as comfortable as you can be in this position."

"I'm fine." Fire burned in her eyes.

"All right. By the way, do you know how gorgeous you look restrained and open to whatever I want to do?" He reached down and removed the cock harness. His dick bounced with freedom. She licked her lips, but he ignored her. "Time for more fun."

Tyler walked to the end of the lounger and climbed between her legs. "Now, my sweet, I'm going to lick you until you go wild, and I can taste your sweet cream."

She groaned as Tyler went to work. Her sweet and spicy flavor hit his tongue, and he licked, sucked, and tongue-fucked her. It didn't take long until her body responded, and she orgasmed against his lips.

Sitting back, he checked her feet. They were warm. Good. He bathed her body once again, bringing her back down to earth a bit. He also checked her wrists. "Arms okay? No numbness?"

"None."

"Perfect." He grabbed another toy.

"What is that?" Her gaze was locked on the item in his hand.

"Oh, this?" He waved the device. "It's called a wand. Basically, a personal massager."

"What are you going to do with it?" She sounded soft and maybe a little bit apprehensive.

"Make you feel good." He knelt beside her hips.

"I'm not sure about this," she said as he placed the wand on her mound.

"I am." He flipped it on the lowest setting. Her mouth dropped open.

"Okay, that's not so bad."

"Just wait." He adjusted the head of the toy against her clit and started the pulsing.

"Shit," she cried out.

"This one has a lot of settings: pulsations, escalations, and waves. I can create about fifty different combinations." He switched to a different pulse. "Also, it has adjustable speeds."

Becca groaned and closed her eyes.

Tyler varied the wand, loving how she would twitch or moan. He kept her on edge for a while, then turned the wand up. "Come for me now, baby."

Her arms jerked in the restraints as her body quivered and she climaxed. Her breath shuddered in and out of her lungs, but he kept the wand on her clit.

"Please." Her words were soft. "Please, do something. My pussy is so empty."

"It is?"

"Stop grinning and do something."

He laughed. "Behave, woman." He slapped her breast, and she groaned. Tyler stretched over her body and grabbed one of the dildos. He twirled it around her entrance. She was soaked.

"Yes, please. Fuck me."

"Be careful what you ask for." He thrust the dildo into her.

She cried out as her muscles closed over the toy, and she orgasmed once again. He didn't move the dildo, just held it in place as he changed the pulsation on the wand.

"Tyler, no. I can't come again." She jerked her arms and legs.

"You can, and you will." He adjusted the wand, and she screamed as she came apart. Her body was in a constant state of arousal. Yet she didn't call her safe word. She was taking everything he had to give. "One more, baby."

"I..." She panted, trying to catch her breath as he changed the vibrations.

Her orgasm this time was longer and stronger. He turned off the wand as Becca slumped against the lounger.

With care, he removed the dildo from her pussy while her body shook with the aftermath of all her climaxes.

"You are so damn beautiful," he whispered before dropping a soft kiss on her lips. Tyler put the toys on the table, then unfastened the restraints.

Her wrists were a little red where she'd strained against their hold, but that was it. He placed her arms over her stomach and then released her legs. "Becca."

"I think I'm dead. I'm floating on a bed of clouds." Her words were barely a whisper.

"I bet you are. Be right back."

"I'm not going anywhere."

Walking on air from making her come so much, Tyler went into the bathroom and filled the tub. He added some essential oils before returning to Becca. She lay in the exact same spot, eyes closed.

"Bath time." He lifted her in his arms and carried her into the bathroom. He stepped in the bath, and lowered them both into the water.

"Nice," she murmured, her body relaxing against his.

"Yes, it is." He picked up a washcloth and began running it over her body. Becca didn't move a muscle. He'd worn his woman out.

His hand froze. *His woman.*

Yes, she was. He had no idea of how he would let her go Sunday, but he had to. This was only for a week, and he'd made the agreement. Besides, she had her dream job to go to. He belonged here at the ranch.

Tyler finished bathing her, and then himself before climbing out with her in his arms. He wrapped a towel around her and carried her to the bed. The second he lay her down, she curled into a ball.

He grinned as a soft snore left her lips, then pulled the covers over her and went to clean up the living room. They had time yet, and he wasn't going to worry about what would happen when she left.

As long as Becca was happy and satisfied, that was good enough for him.

Chapter Fifteen

♥

Becca curled into Tyler's embrace. Her body still hummed from their afternoon activities. He had dinner sent down from the ranch house and fed her in bed. Tyler had tested her boundaries this afternoon, and she'd loved every second of it.

She'd almost called her safe word when he told her one last orgasm, but she didn't. And then it hit, and she floated on a cloud of happiness and satisfaction. *Is this subspace?* She'd never felt so satisfied or loved.

Loved? Yes, loved. Tyler lovingly took care of her body, spirit, and needs. She was falling for him. Her heart pounded. Normally, she'd run a mile from these thoughts but not with Tyler. Becca hadn't protected her heart the way she wanted, and now she was going to pay the price.

No matter how much it hurt.

Tyler's place was here, running the ranch while her life awaited her, with a new job and a fresh start.

"How are you feeling?" he asked as his palms skimmed over her back.

"Wonderful." She tilted her head so she could look at him, his chest hair rough against her cheek. "Can we talk about tomorrow?"

"Yes, but it's your choice on adding Jared to the mix."

"You always say it's my choice, but what about you?" She wanted him to enjoy the experience as well.

"This isn't about me. It's about you. You can have me and Jared, or just me. It's totally up to you."

A small shiver worked its way from her toes to her head. With the plug in her ass as Tyler fucked her, she'd imagined that was how it would be having two men, but she also had the feeling it could be more. "You're sure Jared is okay with this?"

"Yes."

Becca swallowed as excitement filled her.

Isn't this what the week is about, me experiencing everything—including my fantasies?

"All right. I want to do it."

Tyler brushed a kiss over her lips. "You won't regret it."

"I won't." She wouldn't. She wanted to experience two men at once, and she trusted Tyler to know if it would work or not.

"Jared and I will worship your body tomorrow. I set up one of the special cabins for us."

"You did?" She'd read about them when she first got here. The book had only said they were available for couples who wanted more than what their cabins could provide.

"Special for us." He shifted her in his embrace. "How long do you want Jared with us?"

"I'm not sure what you mean."

"I mean, do you want him there the whole day, half a day, or just long enough to take your ass while I fuck your pussy?"

She squirmed as anticipation flowed through her. "I hadn't thought about it." She gazed at Tyler. "I'd like some time alone with you first, but I'm thinking not too long, or I might say to hell with Jared."

Tyler chuckled. "I bet you won't. I want you to know that, tomorrow, Jared and I will push your boundaries."

"I'm sure you will." He wouldn't do anything to hurt her or make her uncomfortable. Even today, he'd stopped when she said her safe word to catch her breath.

"With that in mind..." He gave her a hard kiss before he slipped from the bed.

"What are you doing?" she asked as he picked up his clothes.

"Dressing." He pulled his pants on. "You need to rest for tomorrow, and if I stay, we won't be sleeping."

Becca sat up and stared at him. "I want you to stay."

"I know. There are some things I want you to know tonight and sleep on."

"Okay." Becca climbed off the bed, slipped her robe on, and crossed over to him.

"Tomorrow, Jared and I will be fully in command."

"And you weren't today?" He'd been pretty demanding all afternoon.

"More so tomorrow. We'll use safe words as always. But I need you to be vocal if something feels off or if your arms and legs go numb. Anything off and you tell me."

"I can do that." That meant she had to pay attention to more than the way they made her feel. She'd cross that bridge tomorrow.

"It also means when Jared or I tell you to do something, you do it. No questions, no hesitations."

"Fine." She could do that, couldn't she? She obeyed Tyler without hesitation, and he trusted Jared, and she did too. So yes, she could obey both of them.

"I'll have breakfast sent to you, and you will eat it. You'll need your energy. I want you at the special cabin number two at ten. You and I will play until lunch. We'll take a short lunch break, and then Jared will arrive, and we'll pay until we're done."

Becca nodded, but after being with Tyler all week, she knew he had more to say, so she waited.

"Everything you've learned this week will be explored tomorrow. You and I together have only skimmed the surface. I want you to go into this with your eyes open."

At that moment, she realized how important this was to her. It was the last step in freeing the inner sexual woman. She was ready to fly. "My eyes are open. I want this. Tell Jared he can be with us as long as he wants to be."

He nodded and brushed a kiss over her lips. "The path and cabin are clearly marked. You are not to masturbate. Wear your robe and slippers, but nothing else. Oh, please braid your hair."

Anticipation heated her blood. At least she'd have a robe on if she met anyone on her way to the cabin. Becca was grateful for that.

"The cabin door will be unlocked. Enter, remove your robe and slippers. There will be a massage table. You are to climb on it, face down. From that moment on, you are no longer in control. It will be Jared and I."

"I understand." Damn if that didn't make her hot, thinking about both men commanding her.

"I hope you do."

Becca brushed her fingers over the frown on his forehead. Her heart contracted at his serious tone. Tyler's protective instincts were in full force, and it touched her deeply. "I want to do this. For myself. And for you."

He captured her hand and brought it to his mouth. "This is for you. Until tomorrow." Letting go, he turned and marched out of the cabin.

Becca giggled the second the door closed. Tomorrow would be another fantasy come true. Too bad she couldn't make the fantasy of her staying with Tyler a reality. It wasn't possible, and she had to accept it.

She closed her eyes, trying to picture what was going to happen tomorrow, and her body reacted. That's what she needed to concentrate on: tomorrow.

Imagination was something she could control. Reality could wait.

Chapter Sixteen

♥

The next morning, Becca swallowed her nervousness as she stood before cabin two. Her body hummed with excitement and need. She'd slept fairly well, considering her erotic dreams. And while she hadn't felt like eating this morning, she ate the full breakfast Tyler had sent to her cabin. She'd showered, shaved, and done everything to be ready for today, including shoring up her mental readiness after faltering several times.

She wanted this.

She needed this.

Her freedom required this.

Sucking in a breath, Becca turned the doorknob and walked into the cabin. She stopped in the doorway and leaned against it for support because... *Holy cow*. Before her lay a... *So this must be a real BDSM dungeon. Not even in my wildest dreams...*

Rings were mounted into the walls, ceiling, and floor, some of them with chains attached. She turned her head. Three cabinets, but only one was open. She could see vibrators, plugs, lotions, and other toys.

What was in the two closed cabinets? A tremor swept through her body.

"You can do this."

Saying the words out loud helped stiffen her spine. She wanted to do this. To get past the last of her inhibitions.

She removed her slippers and put them off to the side of the door, then removed her robe and hung it on the coat rack. Becca shivered as the cool air brushed her skin. She probably wouldn't be cold for long.

The massage table sat to the left of a bench. Becca padded over and glanced around the room. Where were Tyler and Jared? She couldn't see anyone, but she had a feeling they were watching her from somewhere.

Carefully, she sat on the blanketed massage table and then laid down on her stomach. She folded her arms and rested her cheek against her hands before closing her eyes. Time seemed to stop as she laid there waiting.

It could have been a minute or five before she heard footsteps. She didn't shift from her position. No matter how much she wanted to see who it was, she'd wait. She jumped when warm fingers trailed up her spine.

"Easy, my pet." Tyler's deep voice penetrated her thoughts and eased her trepidation.

Taking a deep breath and letting it out helped her relax.

"Safe words are green, yellow, and red," he added.

"Yes, Sir." The *sir* slipped out naturally.

"I'm going to prepare you for today. I want you to talk to me as I do so. Tell me how you're feeling. How excited you are. If anything scares you, or if you hurt anywhere. No holding back on anything. I want to know everything."

"Yes, Sir." She'd used her voice this week, but today, everything thing felt different. Sharper and more real.

She heard a soft *snick,* then the smell of vanilla reached her senses. Tyler placed his hands on her shoulders and started massaging.

"Umm, feels good." It did. She loved his full-body massages. By the time he finished, Becca wasn't sure if she could move—or if she even wanted to.

"Time for a shower." Tyler helped her off the table.

"I didn't see a bathroom when I walked in." But she hadn't been paying that much attention to anything but the main room.

"It's here." He guided her over to the back wall. The door was inset so she'd missed it. He pushed it open. The bathroom held a sink, toilet, and an obscenely big shower. "Let me put your hair up so it doesn't get wet." He found a clip, lifted her braid, and attached it to the top of her head, before he secured a shower cap over her hair.

He opened the shower door and guided her through, then closed the door with a click. It was then she realized Tyler was already naked. How had she not noticed that before now? Maybe because she was used to him running around her cabin without clothing.

Turning, she looked around the shower. Maybe that wasn't the right word; this wasn't like any shower she'd ever been in. There were water jets everywhere, as well as several hand-held shower heads.

In the corner, there were shelves that held soap, shampoo, and a couple of different looking sponges. There was a bench that ran the length of the shower on one side and a smaller one in the back.

"Here we go," he said as he touched a small panel next to the door. The water flowed from one of the handhelds in a small trickle at first, then stronger. The cool water touched her toes, and he stuck his hand under the flow before touching the panel.

"That should be perfect." He put his arms around her waist and guided her forward as the jets kicked on.

"Oh my goodness." It was like being under several waterfalls at once. The water flowed over her shoulders, her arms, her hips and legs. It wasn't pulsing or anything, just gentle like rain.

Tyler turned her in his arms, and the water caressed her back. When he reached behind her, she started to turn her head.

"No peeking." He captured her chin with his free hand.

"Okay." She kept her gaze on his chest as she waited.

What she guessed was the sponge touched her shoulder blade. Tyler guided it over her back, down her spine, and over her ass. Goosebumps spread over her skin. He caressed every inch of her backside before he turned her in his arms.

She leaned against him, feeling his hard cock between their bodies. He bathed her collarbone, her breasts, and she moaned as he cupped her. Tyler placed the sponge over her nipples, and it began to vibrate.

"What the heck?" She stiffened in his arms.

"Vibrating sponge," he whispered, sliding his palm to her belly.

"You and your vibrators." Becca relaxed back into his hold. She enjoyed having Tyler bathe her. It was something she'd never thought of before this week.

His hand slid over her belly to the top of her mound. "Lift your right leg and place it on the bench."

Becca blinked. On the bench? It took her a moment to follow his order.

"You were a little slow."

"Sorry, Sir. It took me a second to understand your directions."

He chuckled, lowering his hand farther. Her hips shifted as he dove between her thighs. The vibrations seemed much stronger now. He slid the sponge down until the soft material touched her clit.

Her pussy tightened, and her mouth opened on a breathless moan. Arousal coursed through her. Tyler pressed the sponge against her, and rough nubs teased her clit. If he kept that up, she was going to come way too fast. She shifted.

"Be still." His free hand swatted her wet ass, and she almost lost her footing. Yet as the stinging sensation flowed through her body, it kicked her arousal up a notch.

When he swirled the vibrations around her clit, her belly tightened.

Damn. After everything they'd done this week, she didn't think she would be so sensitive, but she was. She wasn't going to be able to hold her climax back for long.

"I'm going to come."

"You may come, baby."

Her body shuddered in his arms as her climax hit. It wasn't a long one, thank goodness, but it still made her knees weak. He removed sponge and she breathed a sigh of relief, only to cry out as it was replaced by pulsating water.

"I said be still." His voice was rough in her ear.

"But…" Her voice trailed off as he pushed a finger into her pussy. Damn the man. She pressed against his finger, which only moved the pulsating water closer. "You're driving me crazy."

"That's my job." The water was aimed at her clit, and Tyler curved his finger to hit her G-spot.

Her knees shook, and she grabbed Tyler's arms to keep from falling. The water was removed, and he slid his finger from her pussy. He wrapped his arms around her waist and held her until her body stopped shaking.

If this was how the day was going to go, she would be a mess before noon.

He lifted her leg off the bench, allowing the warm water to wash over both of them. When her breathing returned to normal, Tyler shut the water off and guided her out of the shower.

Using a towel from the warming rack, he dried her body, and removed the shower cap before he took care of himself. Slight tremors still went through her body, but at least she could stand.

"So perfect." Tyler gave her a quick kiss. "Go into the other room and wait for me."

She opened her mouth to protest, but his glare reminded her to obey him. Strange how that didn't bother her. She nodded and left the bathroom. She gasped as she entered the main room to see Jared standing on the other side of the room, naked.

Unable to help herself, her gaze roamed over his body. He was muscular, like Tyler, but... Then, unable to hide her curiosity, she stared at his cock. He looked slightly larger than Tyler; how was that possible? And how would that cock feel in her ass?

Her breathing increased. Did she really want to do this? Oh, yeah. It was a one-time fantasy, and why not? They were all consenting adults.

"Come here." Jared's voice was low and deep.

Swallowing hard, Becca walked over to Jared, her heart pounding.

"So beautiful." Jared's hands rose and covered her breasts, caressing them gently. His touch was different from Tyler's. Jared's skin was softer, maybe because he worked in the office and the lodge? Tyler worked with the horses and outside. Jared pinched her nipples.

Becca gasped.

"So responsive too."

She didn't know what to say and started to lower her gaze.

"Oh no, keep your eyes up and straight ahead." Jared shifted positions and was no longer in front of her.

She focused on the wall. The air was heavy with anticipation.

His fingers returned to her nipples, then a slight pinch and the coldness of a chain against her stomach. Okay, nipple clamps. She could handle them. But why did the chain hang so low?

"You are so perfect," he whispered, his hands on her shoulders, guiding her backward.

The back of her knees hit something hard, and Jared gently coaxed her to a sitting position, then she reclined slightly. Becca kept her gaze straight ahead even as excitement flowed through her. She'd seen the chair, but hadn't paid that much attention to it.

Jared knelt in front of her. His fingers caressed the outside of her thighs before sliding to her ankles. He lifted her foot, placed it on a small ledge, and buckled a padded restraint around it.

Oh boy, this was expected, yet unexpected. He did the same thing with her other leg. Cool air teased her pussy. His hands touched the inside of her thighs, and he pressed them outward. Her breath caught in her throat. When Jared pressed her thighs wide, the seat reclined more.

"Perfect." Straps were placed above her knees, holding her in place, though she still had her hands and arms free.

Becca could barely breathe. What were these two planning? She wasn't afraid, just curious and excited and anticipating their next move.

"Arms over your head."

She didn't hesitate and lifted her arms, allowing him to further restrain her. Jared was very careful, she noticed. Just like with her ankles, he ran his finger between her skin and the restraint, making sure there was enough room.

"Damn, you do good work," Tyler commented.

Becca turned her head to see Tyler lounging in the doorway. His expression showed appreciation and desire heated his gaze.

"I told you to leave this to me."

Tyler pushed away from the doorframe, and her breath hitched in her throat. There was a possessive gleam in his eyes that sent a shot of excitement through her veins, and there was something in that gleam that told her she was in for one hell of a ride.

"Eyes on me," Tyler ordered as he stepped between her open thighs.

It was difficult to keep her gaze on his face as the chain moved and tugged the clamps on her nipples.

"I think these might need to be tighter." Becca whimpered as he tightened each one in turn. Her nipples were on fire, and pleasure coursed directly to her clit. Her pussy clenched over and over again. Oh man, these two were really going to put her through the paces today. But she could handle them. She hoped.

"That's better, don't you think, Jared?"

"Much better. Her body is so responsive."

Becca kept her gaze on Tyler's face, but she could feel his hand, and when he shifted on his feet, his hard cock brushed against her entrance.

"Look down, Becca."

She glanced down and barely prevented a gasp. She hadn't realized how wide open she was. Her nipples were hard in the clamps, and the chain trailed over her belly to... a cock ring. Tyler's cock ring was attached to the chain between her breasts. "Oh, Lord," she whispered.

"I don't want to move. Jared, see if she's wet."

Jared chuckled, leaned over, and pushed his finger into her pussy. "Oh yeah, she's wet." Becca knew she was. Very.

"Good."

She held her breath as Jared removed his finger. What was Tyler planning? She didn't have long to wait. He plunged his cock into her pussy.

"Ahhhh." The surprise of the unexpected move caused her to push against the restraints. She wanted to grab his shoulders. He pulled out and plunged in again. The chain tugged, and she dropped her head back against the cushion as sensations coursed through her.

Tyler thrusted in and out until he was fully seated in her pussy. Her mouth lay open as she tried to catch her breath. He then tugged the chain, and she lost what little breath she had.

"Remember the rules. Talk to us."

"You're both going to kill me," she panted.

"You say that a lot. But we'd never kill you." He pulled nearly out, then slid back into her, his balls hitting her ass.

"Do you have any idea of how it feels to have you fucking me and those clamps pulling on my nipples at the same time?"

"No. Tell us." Again, he pulled back, then plunged into her.

"It's arousing, erotic, and downright thrilling. My clit is throbbing in time with my nipples. My pussy is clenched around your cock. There's lightning flowing through my veins, making my nerves dance."

Each stroke was slow and deliberate. Becca wondered where Jared was. She couldn't see him, but she sensed he was behind her, watching. Her eyes drifted shut.

"No!" Tyler yelled. Her eyes opened. "You will watch. Watch me fuck you." With those words, he began to piston in and out of her, his cock now shiny with her juices.

Her nipples stung with each tug, and a flutter started in her gut, slow but building fast. "I'm going to come."

"Then come, baby. Cream all over me."

Her pussy trembled before it clenched around his cock, and her orgasm took her breath away. Her body shook in the restraints. Tyler never stopped moving. It was difficult for her to keep her eyes open, but she did. And she watched his cock disappear into her, only to reappear. Another climax built.

"Now, Jared," Tyler said.

Now what? She'd barely registered the thought when Jared's palm covered her stomach, and his index finger pressed her clit.

"Oh fuck." She tugged at her bonds to no avail.

"Easy, baby, it's just a finger vibrator."

Becca mumbled under her breath about men and their vibrators. Jared teased her clit with the toy. Damn if it wasn't like someone shot liquid fire through her body, running from her pussy to her clit to her nipples and back again.

"Come for us again, baby."

She did. Her body shook with another climax. What was that? Number three or four? She couldn't remember. Becca panted; they had to be done with her by now. But Tyler grinned at her and nodded.

Jared kept pressing on her clit as Tyler gave one last hard thrust into her pussy. Her orgasm continued to shoot through her, and she wasn't prepared when the nipple clamps were removed. Even with their warm mouths on each breast, the blood flowing back to her nipples created ripples through her body.

Becca bucked against the restraints. Her pussy tightened around Tyler's cock, trying to milk him, but he didn't come. Finally, her body stopped shaking, and she collapsed against the chair.

Somewhere in her orgasmic haze, Jared had removed his finger from her clit. She closed her eyes as she caught her breath.

"Open your eyes."

She obeyed Tyler's firm command and watched as he pulled his engorged cock from her. Her pussy clenched, feeling empty.

"You're amazing." Tyler brushed a kiss over her lips before he stepped away from her.

Jared took his place, holding a washcloth. He bathed her body and her pussy before drying her off. Tyler tended to himself. Together, they released her from the restraints and massaged her arms and legs.

"Okay, baby?" Tyler asked.

"Yes."

"Good." Both men then pressed kisses over her face, neck, and shoulders as they helped her stand. Tyler kept his arms around her waist as Jared moved the chair out of the way.

What did they have in mind next? How much more could she take? Her pussy twitched. Jared pulled over a lounger like the one she and Tyler had used in her cabin.

"Lay down on your back," Tyler said.

Once she'd done that, Tyler began positioning her the way her wanted her. Her ass was at the top of the curve, her legs dangling. Her head was against the top of the lounger. Since there was no cushion, if she wanted to see what they were doing, she'd have to raise her head.

Wait a second. This lounger was shorter than the one they used yesterday. Restraints were fastened around her feet, spreading her wide once again, but they left her hands free. The *pop* of a top sounded loud in the room.

Cool lube teased her ass. Tyler used his finger to lube her up and then there was pressure against her ass. She forced herself to exhale and relax. The toy slipped into her ass, then was pulled out only to be pushed in once again.

This didn't feel like a plug. It was something small, beads almost...oh crap anal beads. Tyler moved into her line of sight.

"You have a choice to make. Jared can fuck you while you suck me off, or I can fuck you while you suck him off."

Becca turned her head, seeing Jared standing there, his cock engorged. "I want to suck Jared." She wanted to see how Jared tasted and how much he could take. Tyler leaned down and brushed a kiss over her lips.

"I'm putting a scarf in your right hand, if something becomes too much, drop it, and we'll stop."

"Yes, Sir." His eyes flared with fire before he moved away. A piece of soft material was pressed into her right palm, and she closed her fingers around it.

"Let's make a quick adjustment," Jared said, standing at her head. Before she could comprehend what he meant, they shifted her body so her head was fully tilted back, and Jared's dick was close to her lips. "Much better."

She took a deep breath and opened her mouth, only to release a squeal when Tyler filled her on the first thrust.

Jared's cock nudged her lips, and she licked the head. He tasted a bit saltier than Tyler.

Jared slid into her mouth as Tyler started moving. So different. Two men at once. Jared was careful as he moved in and out of her mouth, not going too deep, whereas Tyler stroked in and out of her pussy with more force.

Becca wanted to concentrate on both men, but it was difficult, so she decided to do her best to concentrate on Jared. She lifted her left hand and caressed his balls. They felt smooth and somewhat firm.

Each of the men's thrusts ratcheted her own need higher. She never imagined having two men like this. A sense of power flowed through her. She wanted to make them come. She wanted them on their knees, shaking in the aftermath of their orgasms as they had done to her.

She licked and sucked Jared's cock, wishing she could see his face. The scent of sex was strong, and both men's breathing had increased. So had hers. Becca had to remember to breathe through her nose.

Tyler stroked faster, and her body tightened. No, she didn't want to be the first one to climax. She concentrated on Jared, sucking him deep while her fingers toyed with his balls.

"I'm going to come." Jared's voice was strained.

His body stiffened, his essence filled her mouth, and she swallowed, pleased she'd made him come first. He pulsed for what felt like several minutes before he pulled his cock from her mouth.

Jared was breathing hard as he stepped back and grinned at her before he leaned over and kissed her, hard and deep. "I love tasting my desire on your lips," he whispered.

Before she could react, Tyler picked up speed. Oh, yeah, she wasn't going to last long. His fingers moved to the toy in her ass, and he began to remove it slowly.

Oh, my God. She'd been concentrating so hard on Jared she hadn't noticed before that the toy was like little balls. And as he pulled one out, her body tightened around the toy and his cock. She started to climax after he pulled three of the balls from her ass.

"Damn, baby." Tyler gasped as he slammed into her pussy. "You are so tight around me." He pulled on the toy.

"*Ahhhh!*" She couldn't catch her breath as he continued to fuck her and removed the toy from her. As he pulled the last ball from her ass, he plunged into her and climaxed.

Becca laid there shaking as her body slowly recovered from the orgasm. She hadn't expected the toy he'd used. As her breathing became more normal, Jared slipped his hands and forearms under her shoulders and lifted her.

Tyler leaned over and kissed her before he pulled his cock from her body. He was grinning as he held up the toy. "Anal beads."

Becca rolled her eyes. Leave it to him to find a toy they hadn't used. Then again, there were so many they hadn't tried. Tyler released her legs, but she couldn't move. The men bathed her and then cleaned themselves while she just laid there, having no idea if she'd ever move again.

"Shall we move on?" Tyler asked.

"By all means," Jared said. "I'm enjoying myself."

Her gaze traveled from one man to the other. They both wore devilish grins.

Oh boy, I'm in for it.

That statement couldn't have been truer. They continued to torment her until lunch time, at which point, she wasn't sure she had the strength to eat.

Tyler fed her from his plate, while Jared rubbed her shoulders and arms. After they finished eating, they took a short break and chatted. Then they were at it again. Her body didn't hurt but was super sensitive from their touch. After yet another climax, they moved her to the bed while they grabbed something made of leather.

She laid there, watching them connect carabiners to ceiling hooks. When they were done, she realized they had hung some sort of leather swing. Tyler walked over to the bed and extended is hand to her.

Becca took a deep breath and allowed Tyler to help her up and guide her over to the swing, where Jared stood.

"We've set this up so we can fuck you together." Tyler held her close. "Jared in your ass and me in your pussy."

Even though she knew this was going to happen, apprehension coursed through her. She trusted Tyler, and Jared as well. Otherwise, she wouldn't have agreed to this.

She blew out a breath as she eyed the swing. "Okay, how are we doing this?"

"Let us do all the work." Tyler stood behind her, put his hands under her ass, and lifted her.

Jared slipped the leg straps on her so they would support her at the back of her knees, then he positioned a brace behind her so she wouldn't fall if she leaned back. Another brace behind her shoulders and she was perfectly suspended.

"Put your hands on the bar," Tyler said.

Becca looked up at the bar above her head and placed her hands on it. Tyler released her, and she was suspended in air.

"How does it feel?" Tyler asked.

"Different."

"I bet," Jared commented, giving the swing a little push.

Her hands tightened on the bar as she swung back and forth.

"Let's get ready." Tyler tossed Jared a foil packet. Condom. She released another breath. Tyler had talked to her about this. While Tyler would be bare, Jared would wear a condom.

She was on birth control, and Tyler provided her his and Jared's last medical reports.

Tyler tossed Jared a bottle of lube. Becca gulped, then took a deep breath.

Okay, I can do this. Hell, I want to do this. To feel both men take her at the same time.

"Get out of your head," Tyler said, pressing her legs apart in the supple leather and stepping between them.

"I'm trying." Her mind swirled over how this would work. She shifted when she felt Jared's fingers pressing against her ass. Her hips moved forward as if to get away from his touch.

"Easy, baby." Tyler was there, hands on her hips to steady her. "Talk to me."

"I don't know what to say." Jared's finger penetrated her anus, and she couldn't help but tighten against it. "I'm nervous. I want this, but I'm nervous."

"Relax," Jared bit out.

"I'm trying." She really was, but something inside her rebelled.

"Look at me." Her gaze met Tyler's. "Breathe in and now breathe out."

Becca did as he instructed. After several breaths, she felt calmer.

"Good. I'm here. You're not alone; you have your safe words, if you need them. If you want to stop, just safeword."

"Okay." She bit her lip as Jared slipped a third finger into her ass. When had he put in the second one? Her ass opened to him. Jared pumped his fingers in and out, adding lube.

"How does it feel, baby?" Tyler asked.

"Good. Jared's fingers are loosening up my ass, and it feels good."

"Perfect."

Jared removed his fingers, replaced by the head of his cock.

Becca held her breath.

"It will be fine." Tyler reached behind her and pulled her ass cheeks apart. "I'm here. Jared's here. You are special. This is all for you, Becca. Breathe out and push out."

She released her breath and did as Tyler said.

Jared's cock pushed forward. "Damn," she whispered. "He feels a hell of a lot bigger than you."

Jared chuckled.

"He's not." Tyler caressed her ass as Jared worked his cock into her.

Becca closed her eyes as goosebumps spread over her skin while Jared pushed past the ring of muscle. There was a slight burning sensation, but it faded quickly. Soon, Jared was buried in her ass.

Tyler devoured her mouth as his fingers found her clit. It only took a quick touch, and her clit was hot and hard. It took a second for her to realize something was different.

"Tyler?" she asked when he broke the kiss.

"Just some warming gel to make the experience more intense." He stepped back.

More intense? Hell, she was past intense. Jared's palms were on her inside thighs, his chest against her back. The leather of the swing felt warm against her skin while it left her body open to the two men.

Tyler's cock pressed against her entrance. Now she understood why Jared held her, to keep her from swinging.

Her breathing quickened as Tyler continued to see-saw in and out until half of his cock was buried. Becca's heart pounded. She felt full. Even when Tyler used the dildo on her ass and fucked her, it hadn't felt like this.

Was the human body made for this? She couldn't catch her breath as Jared removed his hands from her thighs, and Tyler gripped her waist. There was a single heartbeat, and then Jared slid back, and Tyler moved forward.

They set a slow, easy pace, neither ever fully pulling out. One in and one out. Tension built in her as they continued. Her mind tried to process all the sensations washing through her body as her clit grew warmer and pulsed.

"How you doing, baby?" Tyler asked as he slid into her pussy.

"Green. This is... I can't find the right word." And she couldn't.

"So tight," Jared whispered. "But so fucking sexy."

"Yeah," Tyler commented. "I can feel your dick with every stroke."

"Me too."

Their words made her blood sing. They picked up the pace of their thrusting until she trembled with desire. "Please, fuck me," she whispered. Her hands clenched and unclenched on the bar. She needed to come.

One hand, she could hold on with one hand. Tyler captured her hand as she lowered it. "Hold on to the straps." At his commanding tone, she curled her fingers back around the leather material.

Jared cupped her breasts and began to pluck at her nipples. How much more? She stared at the ceiling.

"Please." She was begging and didn't care. "Fuck me. I want it all."

"We will."

"You're killing me. I need both of you. Now." Her body was on the precipice of something special, something she'd never felt before. "I'm right there; push me over."

Jared fingers pinched her nipples as Tyler's lips caressed her neck, as his tongue licked the sweat from her skin.

"Ready, Jared?" Tyler asked.

"Oh, yeah."

She cried out as both men began pistoning in and out of her. Jared continued to pluck and pinch her nipples. Her clit was on fire. She wanted more.

She wasn't sure how she could want more, but she did.

Even with Tyler's hands on her hips, she was able to shift slightly to push her pelvis down onto his cock even more. God, she was so full. Two cocks in her, stretched beyond what she thought she could take.

Tremors rolled through her body. Totally unexpected, her climax flashed and she cried out as it flashed through her veins. But it didn't help. She was still waiting to fall over the cliff.

"More," she whispered.

"Hold on," Tyler said.

Her fingers tightened on the leather strap as the two men moved even faster. Her head lolled back. Oh, Lord. She couldn't tell where one stopped and the other started. Her nerves shimmied. Another climax hit her, but it only made her hotter and drove her desire through the roof.

"I need…" She didn't know what she needed.

"I'm almost there." Jared's rough voice sounded in her ear.

"Then let's do this," Tyler said.

She almost asked *do what*, when Tyler's fingers found her clit. One single touch and she screamed as her body convulsed around both men. They shouted as they both slammed into her and found their release.

Becca couldn't catch her breath as her orgasm seemed to go on and on. The men held her between their bodies as they pulsed within her. Their hot, heavy breath brushed over her skin. It could have been hours later, for all she knew, when Jared pulled from her tender ass.

Tyler slipped from her pussy. Together, they removed her from the swing, and Tyler carried her to the bed and laid her gently on the sheets.

"Thank you for letting me be a part of your special day," Jared said. He leaned in, kissed her lips, then moved out of sight.

Tyler gently dried her body and his before he climbed into the bed with her, and pulled her into his arms.

Becca curled into his embrace, her body sated and her mind at peace. She would never forget this for the rest of her life.

***

Tyler laid there with Becca asleep in his arms as Jared cleaned up and left the cabin. He kept his gaze on her.

God, she was... There was more than beauty in her. Here was a woman who embraced who she was. A sensual woman with wants and needs she wasn't afraid to explore anymore.

How the hell will I let her go tomorrow? He'd given his heart to Becca and he wasn't sure he'd survive losing her a second time.

Could I convince her to stay?

That wouldn't be fair to her. She had her dream job waiting.

I could follow her. His gut clenched. Tyler disliked the city, but maybe for Becca he'd try. He didn't have all the answers tonight. He knew one thing for sure.

He'd fallen in love with her.

Chapter Seventeen

♥

The next morning, Becca zipped her suitcase with a sigh. She didn't want to leave. This week had been so eye opening, especially yesterday. After they made love all night, Tyler had left her early this morning with a kiss and a whisper.

"Go live your dreams, sweetheart. You deserve them."

Sweet, loving Tyler. Everything he'd done this week had helped her break free of her inhibitions but also helped her realize how empty her life had been. He was so unselfish, thinking of her pleasure and her needs and sometimes denying his own.

Her dream job awaited her, except right now, at this moment, she wasn't the least bit excited about it. She pulled her suitcase off the bed and wheeled it out of the cabin toward the main gate where her car was parked.

With each step, her heart grew heavier. This wasn't about the fantastic sex they'd had. It had to do with her feelings for Tyler. How could she leave the man she loved? Becca stopped in her tracks. She loved Tyler, crazy as it sounded. Pinpointing when she fell for him was impossible.

She had to talk to Tyler before she left. Tell him what this week had meant to her and how she felt. It would only be right. Stashing her suitcase in her car, she headed for the main house. Her courage grew as she walked.

Loud voices greeted her as she entered. Vic, the cook, was shouting, and Jared yelled back.

Interesting. She headed toward the kitchen where the voices came from.

"It's impossible, Jared. They won't deliver until Tuesday."

"We need that food tonight."

"What do you want me to do?" Vic asked.

"Excuse me. Do you have a problem?" She'd never seen Jared look so frustrated.

"Becca." Jared's eyes lit up. "I thought you'd left already."

"I was about to. Is there something I can help with?" They'd mentioned a food delivery. She knew a lot of food vendors in northern California, since she'd worked with a lot of them.

"Not unless you have some pull with Wilson's Produce Company," Vic muttered.

"I just might. What's the issue?" Her fingers tingled with the idea of solving the problem. For a week now, she'd concentrated on herself, and she missed the business.

"We need the produce this afternoon, but they're insisting they can't deliver until Tuesday." Jared scrubbed his hand through his hair. "We have new guests arriving later today."

Becca frowned. "That shouldn't be a concern." She pulled her cell phone out of her pocket. "Do you mind if I call them?"

"Be my guest."

Becca pulled up her contacts and hit the connect button. "Hey, Rich, Becca here. I'm at the Quick Silver Ranch, and they need their delivery today." She nodded while Rich talked to her about how busy they were and how they were short a driver. Her mind worked on how to fix the problem and came up with a possibility. "I see. Hold on for a second."

She tapped the mute button and looked at Jared. "They say they're shorthanded on drivers today, so they're only making the large deliveries. If you double the order, I'm positive I can get them to deliver, unless you want to pick it up yourself?"

Jared looked at Vic, who shook his head. "I don't have anyone to go pick it up. Double it. If you have to, triple it; we can use whatever you can get us," Jared said.

"Rich," Becca said. "Double the order and deliver today." She listened to Rich stumble over his words, and she laughed. "Yes, I know. Thanks so much." Becca hit the off button and looked at the men. "All done, it will be here in about three hours."

"Now what about the other places?" Vic asked.

"Others?" She glanced at Jared's wide grin.

"Want to try your hand at a couple of other places that are giving us issues?" Jared asked.

"I can do that." This was her job, dealing with vendors.

"Come into my office." Jared gestured to the kitchen doors. She exited the kitchen and then followed Jared down the hall to his office. "Please, sit here," he held out his executive desk chair for her.

Becca sank into the luxury leather chair while Jared sat in the overstuffed chair in front of his desk. "There's a list of our vendors. Those with check marks are done, and the other three insist they can't bring us our full delivery today."

Becca ran her finger down the list. She knew most of these vendors and wondered why there were suddenly problems. A puzzle she was going to solve. "What are my parameters?"

"Double or triple the order if needed, but we need supplies today."

"Do you have the storage capacity?" That was a lot of stuff.

"We do. Normally, I don't have more than a week to a week and a half of stuff delivered, but in this situation, we can make it work."

"Got it. Give me an hour."

Jared nodded and left. Becca grabbed a pen, put her cell on speaker, and dialed the first number. This was going to be fun.

***

"You're fantastic," Jared said an hour later when she called him back into his office. "I couldn't get anyone to listen to me."

Becca smiled. "You have to know how to handle them." She'd had so much fun. A week away from what she loved doing and she was right back in the thick of it. "I only had to double one more order, but full orders will be here today. I couldn't nail down exact times."

Jared sat back. "You're a lifesaver. Vic was ready to quit."

"You need to let Vic work in the kitchen and find someone to handle the ordering and delivering of food." It only made sense since the ranch provided meals, including ones delivered to the cabins.

"I need a head of catering." Jared stared at her. "The job's open if you want it."

Becca blinked in shock. A job at the ranch? That meant she could stay. But did Tyler want her to stay? "I'm not sure."

"Why not?" Jared leaned forward. "You enjoyed yourself here this week, and this would allow you to stay. I need someone I can trust, and I think that's you."

It made sense, but could she risk her heart and her livelihood? "Do you need to talk this over with Tyler first?"

"Not in this case. I handle the employees in the ranch house; he deals with the personnel who work with the animals."

I guess it wouldn't hurt to hear Jared out. "Let's discuss what you want."

***

Tyler groomed the horse after his long ride. He'd said his good-byes to Becca that morning and then took off on Thunder. He couldn't watch her leave. His heart hurt too much.

Maybe he should have told her he loved her, but they'd agreed to the one week. Her dream job waited for her. She'd said that multiple times, so it had to be important to her. Plus, she'd come here after a breaking her engagement, though she seemed to be recovered from that.

Last night, after they made love, he'd been so close to asking her to stay. Then he had to spoil it by asking about her the job. Her eyes lit up as she talked about it, and he wouldn't stop her from chasing her dreams. He wanted her to be happy.

Tyler blew out a breath and rubbed his abs. He'd survive, somehow. Glancing at his watch, he saw it was almost time for the new guests to arrive, and Jared liked him to be around for any questions. He needed to put on a smile and be the host Jared needed.

He walked slowly from the barn to the main house and up to his rooms. Already, the ranch seemed empty without Becca. She lit up his entire world with her smile. She trusted him when she didn't have a reason to trust anyone. How could he let her go without telling her how much she meant to him? He should call her. He'd do that once he finished his duties with the new guests.

Maybe he could figure out something where he would be able spend weekends in San Francisco with her. Would she be willing to have a long-distance romance? God, he hoped so, because he couldn't imagine his life without her. He was a complete goner.

The city wasn't that far away. But was that fair to Jared? They'd gone into this as a partnership. If he was gone every weekend, that left a lot to Jared. Screw it. Jared would understand. After taking a quick shower and pulling on some clothes, he was no closer to an answer.

He'd talk to Jared after dinner with the new guests tonight. Tyler had learned a hard lesson about chasing a woman. That hadn't ended well, yet here he was, ready to do it all over again.

He loved Becca. That had to mean something, and every ounce of his being told him he needed to take this chance. Confusion swirled inside him as he tried to figure a way he could be with Becca and not leave Jared in the lurch. Maybe he could get one of his workers to take over his duties with the horses on weekends, and stay at the ranch on weekdays. That way, he could spend time with Becca.

Could he be happy in the city? With Becca in his arms, yes. With a plan in mind, he descended the stairs. Jared would probably agree, but how did Becca feel? They'd never really confessed their feelings to each other.

He swore silently. He should have told her of his love this morning instead of letting her go. It wasn't too late. Instead of calling her, he'd drive to the city after dinner. He loved her and he would see if she loved him too. It was a risk, but one he was willing to take.

At the bottom of the stairs, he heard the chatter of the new guests. Despite his heavy heart, he pasted on a smile and walked into the dining room. His heart stopped. Becca stood there, speaking with a guest, looking like she'd been part of the ranch staff for months. What was she doing here? She should have been gone hours ago.

"Great," Jared said. "Everyone, this is Tyler, my business partner."

"Becca?" Tyler ignored Jared.

"Hi there." Her sweet voice teased his senses.

"Perfect," Jared said. "I was just about to introduce everyone to our newest team member" Jared walked over to Becca and placed a hand on her shoulder.

"Newest member?" Why was Jared touching his woman? *Pull in the reins*, the sane voice inside him chanted. Jared was his friend, and Becca's gaze was still on Tyler.

"Yes." Becca grinned. "Hi, everyone, I'm Becca, and I'm the head of catering, so if there is anything special you need foodwise, let me know."

Everyone welcomed her and returned to chatting amongst themselves.

Tyler walked over to where Becca and Jared stood grinning. "If you'll excuse us for a minute," Tyler said to his friend.

"Of course." Jared removed his hand and took his seat at the table.

"I thought you'd left," Tyler said, staring down at her beautiful face and ignoring everyone else in the room.

"I was about to and came to ask Jared where you were. I—I needed to talk to you before I left."

"And he offered you a job? What about your dream job?"

"Vic and Jared were having issues with some vendors, and I helped them out." She lifted her hands to his face. "Tyler, something changed in me this week. Something big, and you made that happen. I realized I don't need a dream job, not when I've found the man of my dreams. That is, if he'll have me?"

Becca bit her lower lip. Tyler knew that meant she was unsure of herself. Her words filtered in, filling his heart and soul with overflowing joy. "Want you? I'm never letting you go." He swept her into his arms.

"I love you, Tyler. I won't hold it back anymore."

"I love you too." He hugged her, happiness surging through his veins. "I was going to drive to the city tonight to find you and tell you that. To see what we could work out. And here you are, my dream come true. I can't live without you, Becca."

She beamed. "The universe is looking out for us."

"Yes." He glanced around the room. "If you all will excuse us. I need want some private time with my woman." He guided Becca from the room to rousing applause.

"Your woman?" she asked.

"Yes." He led her out onto the front porch and slanted his mouth over hers.

"Mine," he said. "Now, and forever."

***

Thank you for reading Broken Rules. The companion story Tangled Temptation (Jared and Angie's book) will be released in June. You can preorder now or get it from my direct sale store on my website: www.marietuhart.com

Coming in August will me the first book One Wicked Weekend in my new series Fantasies Inc., will release. In October Decoding Emma the second book will release. To

keep up-to-date you can join my newsletter at: https://w
ww.marietuhart.com/join-mailing-list.html

About the author

♥

Marie Tuhart lives in the beautiful Pacific Northwest with her two dogs, Tommy and Trina. Marie brings to life contemporary approachable alpha heroes and the spunky women who take them to task. Her high-heat, emotional books, many with BDSM elements, inviting the reader to slid the silky scarves between their fingers, fell the kiss of a flogger on their flesh in breathless anticipation of what or who will come next. Embrace the temptation and enjoy a happily ever after that's always about the heroine.

Check out Marie's website at: https://www.marietuhart.com

Other Books by Marie Tuhart

♥

Tempt (Wicked Sanctuary Series)

Entice (Wicked Sanctuary Series)

Seduce (Wicked Sanctuary Series)

Ravish (Wicked Sanctuary Series)

Possess (Wicked Sanctuary Series)

Tantalize (Wicked Sanctuary Series)

Edged (Wicked Sanctuary Series)

Unmasked (Wicked Sanctuary Series)

Too Hot (Wicked Sanctuary Series)

Wicked Sanctuary Novellas:

Untamed

Power Play

Claiming Rose

Standalone Books:

Embracing Desire

Broken Rules

Tangled Temptation

Preview of Tangled Temptation

♥

I'm pathetic. Angie Davidson sat at the table and watched her best friend, Becca, and her husband, Tyler, enjoy the bride and groom dance. It had been six months since Becca's trip to the ranch and reconnecting with Tyler. Quick Silver Ranch never looked more beautiful to her, with the large flower-laden pavilion tents shading the guests from the sun. The place was filled with joy, laughter, and love.

And she was jealous.

Jealous of Becca finding her man, jealous of losing her best friend, and jealous of everyone's happiness. Angie knew that wasn't fair, but it was how she felt. Heck, she was the one who sent Becca to the ranch where she found Tyler, her previous lover.

Angie had spent the last two days at the ranch helping Becca prepare for her wedding. Not that she hadn't enjoyed herself—she had. But with that fun came the realization that her best friend was now living at the ranch, a two-hour drive from her.

Not really far, but there would be no more late-night calls to go out for ice cream, impromptu window shopping, and Angie would be alone in San Francisco. She was truly happy for her friend, very happy, but loneliness had begun to settle in, and she hated it.

She hated it as a kid at the orphanage—until she was adopted. She hated it as a teenager since her adopted brothers were all older. She was always the one standing alone, never picked for anything, and never fitting in. As she got older, she appreciated her adoptive parents and brothers.

At least with Becca, she had a friend she could share a bottle of wine with, go out to the movies or dinner, or just watch chick flicks and cry.

Someone she could discuss sex with and not feel like an outcast.

She forced her gaze from the happy couple and glanced around the pavilion, only to have Jared Turner amble into her line of sight. At six foot two and with an aura of authority, he stood out among the wedding guests in his tux.

Maybe guests wasn't the right word. Everyone here was an employee of the Quick Silver Ranch except her.

Becca had chosen not to invite her mother—boy, was that a long story— and Tyler had no family. Besides, Becca had told Angie the employees of the ranch were her friends, as they had accepted Becca with open arms as the ranch caterer. Angie wondered how it would feel to be part of this special family. Angie hated it when self-pity hit her. She was happy for her friend, but her emotions were a tangled knot in her throat.

Pushing her thoughts away, her gaze traveled over Jared's fine form. She sighed. He was a real man, and he didn't treat her like the indecisive men she'd dated. No. Jared took charge. And it turned her on. Her nipples grew hard every time she saw him.

That was an unusual reaction for her. It was the man himself. In the short time she'd known him, Jared showed the confidence to take anything on. Nothing like the men in her life or at her job. She worked for an accounting firm as an assistant and climbed the company ladder, but somehow along the way, she'd become one of the boys. They all looked to her for decisions and they deferred to her in conversation.

She was tired of it. She wanted a man who would take control, at least for a little while. Jared was the man to do it.

How can I get him to respond to me?

Becca and Tyler were leaving for their honeymoon later today. Angie wasn't expected to return to the city for two weeks. She'd planned it that way. She needed a distraction, something to break her out of this somber mood.

Could I seduce Jared tonight? Well, maybe not quite seduce. The goal was for him to take her to bed and dominate her for the night. She wanted to lie back and enjoy, not do all the work.

A feminine squeal caught her attention, and Angie saw Tyler had dipped Becca low as they danced. Angie grinned. They were so perfect for each other, so in love.

Angie jumped when a masculine hand closed over hers on the table. She tilted her head and saw Jared, his brown eyes twinkling and a grin playing around his sensual lips. Her heart jumped.

Without a word, he pulled her to her feet and out onto the makeshift dance floor.

Yes. Maybe he was attracted to her and maybe seducing him would be easier than she'd thought.

The music had changed. Angie remembered she was the maid of honor, and Jared was the best man; they were required to dance with each other. Her good mood plummeted.

She rested her left hand on his shoulder, and he grasped her right hand, his left hand against her lower back. Blood surged through her veins as they began to waltz. Thank goodness she'd taken dancing lessons years ago. Jared held her close as they danced.

"It's a beautiful wedding," she said and winced at her inane comment.

"Yes." Jared glanced at the couple dancing. "I'm glad I could do something for Becca and Tyler." His voice was whisky smooth.

"They're great together, aren't they?"

"Yes."

Angie stopped talking and drank in the feel of his body against hers as they danced. His hardness to her softness. His hold was the only thing keeping her from melting into a puddle at his feet. She wanted him, so why wasn't she making a move?

Come on, where is that brave, daring woman?

"Becca mentioned you're closing the ranch for a while." She shifted closer to him.

His hand pressed the slightest bit harder on her back as he gazed at her. "Two weeks. We have some renovations to make, and the staff needs some downtime. It works out perfectly with Tyler gone."

"How much can be done in two weeks? When the offices where I work were renovated, it took months." And the workmen came to me to solve problems instead of senior management.

"A lot—if you know how to motivate people."

"Oh?" She tilted her head and fluttered her lashes at him, corny, she knew, but hopefully effective. "And how would you do that?"

He grinned. "Lots of money." He shifted so there was less space between their bodies.

Her fingers trailed over his broad shoulders to his neck. She stroked his dark brown hair. His hand tightened on her lower back, bringing their hips together, his erection firm against her, even with their formal clothing. Yes! Maybe tonight will work out after all.

Angie skimmed her hand from his neck over his back, fingers dancing against his spine, to his well-defined ass. She rested her palm over one cheek and squeezed.

"Behave." His breath brushed her ear as he swatted her ass.

"You hit me!" He actually smacked my ass! Not that it hurt—it hadn't. But now, heat flowed through her veins. How had one little swat made her so hot and needy?

"I'll do worse if you don't behave yourself, Angie."

"Promise?" The word slipped from her before she realized it. The music ended and Jared kept his arm around her waist as he escorted her back to the table and pulled out her chair.

Before she could sit, he cupped her cheeks and tilted her head up. "We'll talk later." He dropped a brief, hard kiss on her lips before he released her and strode away.

Her heart skipped several beats as she watched him cross the room. Her hand rose to her lips as she sank onto the chair. Oh, yeah. If he met her later, there wouldn't be any talking.